SEALED WITH COURAGE

LAURA SCOTT

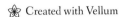

CHAPTER ONE

Aubrey Clark approached the low-income two-story apartment building with trepidation. The East Village suburb of San Diego had the highest crime rate of the metropolitan area. If not for her very real concerns about ten-year-old Lucas Espinoza, and the lack of response from the two phone messages she'd left for his mother, no way would she walk there alone in the dark on a chilly evening in late February.

She shivered, keeping her gaze alert for trouble as she approached the building. No surprise to find the place was in a sorry state of disrepair—peeling paint, sagging eves, several cracked windows, and broken concrete. Aubrey had been there once before to talk about Lucas's progress with learning sign language, but that visit had been during the daytime.

Maybe she should have waited until tomorrow. She'd held her adult sign language class that evening, so she couldn't come until afterward. But tomorrow, though, she could have come right after her kids left for the day, when it was still light out.

Too late to change her mind now. Hesitating on the sidewalk, she peered at the ground-level corner apartment Lucas shared with his mother and her latest boyfriend, Jose.

As a teacher at the school for the deaf, she enjoyed her elementary school kids. Maybe because losing her husband ten years ago meant giving up the idea of having a family of her own. When she'd noticed the bruises on Lucas's arms, she'd used sign language to ask him what had happened. He'd flushed and claimed he'd fallen off his bike.

No way did she believe that. For one thing, she doubted the boy owned a bike as his clothes were threadbare and his shoes were several sizes too big. Second, the bruises had looked to her like fingerprints digging into the boy's skin, not from a fall. She'd tried to ask Lucas about his relationship with Jose, but the child had shaken his head, vehemently denying any trouble.

As required by law, she'd made a report to Child Protective Services. The social worker agreed to investigate Aubrey's concern.

Then Lucas hadn't shown up at school for two days in a row.

She swallowed hard and set her shoulders. Since the start of the school year, Lucas's mother, Nanette Espinoza, had been friendly and seemingly interested in learning sign language so she could communicate with her son. Nanette had come to several of her adult classes, but then she had stopped attending, claiming she had to work.

The bruises Lucas sustained were concerning, but as the social worker had pointed out, they weren't broken bones. She assumed the social worker had seen far worse injuries. Aubrey wanted to believe the child was home with the flu.

But she didn't.

Her steps slowed when she glimpsed movement through the window. A short and burly Hispanic man appeared upset, waving his arms around in anger. Was that Jose? Aubrey found herself moving closer to the window, keeping her gaze focused on his mouth. Initially, she had trouble understanding what he was saying because she could only see his profile. Then he turned just enough that she could read his lips.

You'll tell the police he ran away!

She sucked in a harsh breath. Was he talking about Lucas? Had he done something to the boy? Had he killed him?

Do you want to disappear too?

The man abruptly stopped talking and stared through the window, his gaze colliding with hers. She gasped and quickly ducked down, then belatedly realized what a stupid move that was.

The windows were closed. She should have just waved and pretended to be out for a walk. The man in Lucas's apartment didn't know she could read lips.

A door slammed loudly. Aubrey panicked. Was he coming after her? She jumped up from her crouch and began to run, praying for God to keep her safe.

"Aubrey? Wait! What's wrong?"

A man emerged from the shadows, making her screech in alarm. Then she saw the dog standing beside him.

"Mason?" She recognized Mason Gray and his Belgian Malinois, Bravo. Mason was a former Navy SEAL who was taking her adult sign language class. What he was doing here in East Village was a mystery.

A string of Hispanic curses echoed behind them.

The boyfriend was coming for her!

"Hurry, we need to go!" She instinctively used sign

language as she spoke as Mason was deaf in one ear. She couldn't be sure he'd heard the man's curses.

"Stay to my left," he said curtly. Bravo happened to be on a leash in his right hand, so that worked out fine for her.

Mason broke into a jog. Aubrey did her best to keep up with him, although her idea of running was dashing from the garage to the house to avoid the rain.

As if sensing her difficulty, Mason grabbed her hand and tugged her down one side street, then another. She blindly followed his lead, unfamiliar with this area of the city. She had faith in Mason and Bravo, although she didn't know much about the man other than he used to be a Navy SEAL. He rarely talked about himself, and frankly, he didn't ask anything about her either. All his focus seemed to be centered on learning sign language.

Yet she instinctively trusted him.

It didn't take long for her breathing to grow labored, her heart pounding so hard she thought it might burst out of her chest and land on the road with a squishy plop.

"Can we rest a minute?" she gasped.

Mason didn't answer, so she tugged on his hand. That made him look at her. Since he still held her hand, she used her free hand to spell the word as she spoke. "Rest."

He glanced behind them, then slowed to a walk. Bravo trotted beside him, sniffing the air.

She put a hand to her chest, willing her pulse to return to normal.

"Are you okay?" Mason asked. His gaze was impossible to read in the dark. They slowed so that they could face each other to speak. When they stopped, Mason cocked his right ear toward her to hear better.

"Yes, I am now, but what are you doing here?" She

didn't understand how he'd been there to help. "Do you live in East Village?"

The corner of his mouth quirked in what might have passed for a small smile. "No. I was following you."

"Following me?" She stared at him in shock. "You mean, like a stalker?" The question popped out before she could pull it back.

"Not a stalker, just a concerned citizen." His gaze bored into hers. "I was worried when you left the class and headed this way alone rather than taking your usual path toward your home. What happened back there?"

That he'd paid that much attention to her comings and goings was a discomforting surprise, but his question made her shiver. Now that she was no longer alone, those moments in front of Lucas's house replayed over in her mind.

You'll tell the police he ran away.

Do you want to disappear too?

"I, uh, need to report a missing child to the police." She spoke slowly and loudly so Mason could hear, unwilling to let go of his hand to use sign language. She'd been blessed to have a cochlear implant placed seven years ago, and she'd mentioned the possibility of Mason qualifying for one. He seemed interested, but he had also hoped his hearing would return.

For his sake, she hoped it did too.

He scowled. "Missing child? Who?"

"Lucas Espinoza. He's a ten-year-old boy in my fifth-grade class." She thought about how vulnerable the deaf boy would be if someone had kidnapped him. It would be incredibly difficult for the child to communicate to anyone even if he was able to escape.

Yet she feared Lucas wasn't just missing. If he was, why

the conversation where Jose instructed Nanette to claim he ran away? Why not be honest about the fact that he was missing?

No, she had a very bad feeling Lucas might be dead. Killed by Jose, or someone he knew.

Tears pricked at her eyes. Maybe she shouldn't have reported the bruises to CPS. Maybe she should have tried to talk to Nanette first.

Dear Lord, what had she done?

"Aubrey." Mason gave her hand a tug to get her attention. "What happened to Lucas? How do you know he's missing?"

"I read the man's lips." She recounted how Lucas hadn't shown up for class, so she'd come to talk to the boy's mother when she saw the argument through the window. "He saw me standing outside, and then I heard a door slam. That's when I started running."

Mason's expression turned grim. "Okay, we'll report this to the police, but not until we get you someplace safe."

She nodded, glancing around the dimly lit deserted street. Getting far away from this area seemed reasonable.

Thankfully, Mason continued forward at a slower pace so that she could keep up. Yet as they walked back toward the neighborhood where she lived, she couldn't seem to banish Lucas's face from her mind.

If the boy had been badly hurt, or worse, she'd never, ever forgive herself.

GREAT, *the pretty lady thinks I'm a stalker.* Mason couldn't really blame her since most normal people didn't see danger lurking around every corner.

Then again, his life had been anything but normal.

The fact that Aubrey had been in danger only proved he'd made the right decision in following her. To be fair, he'd have preferred staying in the shadows. But when she'd dropped to her knees, then jumped up and ran, her features alarmed, he'd rushed forward, revealing his position.

Bravo looked up at him, his tongue lolling out of his mouth. The Malinois had been a working dog on their SEAL team. When their last mission had caused Mason's left ear drum to rupture, he'd fought hard to get Bravo retired with him. Thankfully, Bravo was six and a half years old, and they typically retired dogs when they turned seven, so he'd been granted permission to bring his partner home. Still, despite his age, Bravo was the most athletic dog he'd ever worked with, and that short run was nothing compared to the physical exertion he usually offered his partner.

That would have to wait until later. A missing child was serious business. Yet he wasn't comfortable having Aubrey in this section of town. He navigated the streets with her in tow, doing his best to move slowly enough for her to keep up. Since losing the hearing in his left ear, he'd become more attune to his other senses. He could see her chest rising and falling with exertion, sweat dampening her temples where wisps of blond hair escaped from her ponytail. She wasn't conventionally beautiful, her mouth a little too wide, her nose upturned at the end, but that hadn't prevented him from feeling the kick of attraction.

Inappropriate attraction. She was his sign language teacher, nothing more.

When they reached South Park, he paused near a bench and gestured for her to sit down. "We can rest here for a few minutes."

Aubrey dropped gratefully down onto the seat. "I'm

sorry I'm not in better shape," she said loudly enough for him to hear.

He almost said something foolish about how he liked her shape just fine but managed to refrain. No need to live up to his stalker moniker. He sat beside her so that his right ear was closest to her. All those years of keeping Bravo to his right because he happened to be left-handed and held his weapon in his left hand was hampering him now. "Do you often visit your students' homes?"

She winced and shook her head. "No. I just—Lucas is special. He's bright and could do really well for himself in spite of being born deaf. I was hoping to help him obtain a cochlear implant, but now . . ." Her voice trailed off.

"Look, we'll call the police. I'm sure they'll investigate his disappearance." He idly rubbed Bravo's sleek pelt. His K9 partner happened to specialize in tracking scents, but that was when Mason had been a SEAL.

Now he was a civilian trying to adjust to his new injury and his new life.

And doing a piss-poor job at both.

Aubrey put her hand on his arm to get his attention. He noticed she did that a lot, as if she knew firsthand that it was easier to listen when you caught a person's attention first. "Thanks for coming to my rescue."

"No problem, but I am concerned about your safety. Any chance that guy knows where to find you?"

"I don't think so," she said, although her brow puckered in a slight frown. "I personally haven't met Jose, only Nanette, Lucas's mother."

When he'd shown up early for his adult class, he'd noticed the kids called her Ms. Clark. If Lucas happened to mention her name, this Jose guy probably knew who she was. That's how Mason had learned her name even before he'd taken the first sign language class where she'd introduced herself as Aubrey.

A pretty name for a beautiful woman.

He rubbed the back of his neck. Maybe he was a stalker. No question the woman had caught his attention. Not that he'd planned to do anything about it. He was a forty-two-year-old retired SEAL with no clue how to live outside of the navy.

She touched his arm again. "To be honest, I can't say for sure the man in the apartment was Jose. I'm assuming he was Nanette's boyfriend, but he could be anyone."

"Why don't you go ahead and call the police?" he suggested. "The sooner they get out to investigate, the better." After spending twenty-two years doing the most difficult job on the planet, it went against the grain to hand the situation over to the authorities. Of course, he didn't have the credentials to do that work any longer.

Aubrey pulled out her phone. "I've never called 911 before," she said as she hit the buttons.

He listened to her side of the conversation. She was calmer now and gave the information in succinct sentences. Her enunciation was careful, and he'd wondered about her somewhat monotone speech patterns. When he'd learned she'd been born deaf and had been given a cochlear implant, he'd been impressed with how well she'd adapted.

And that she'd continued to dedicate her life to helping those who couldn't hear.

"Thank you," Aubrey finally said. She lowered the phone and touched the end button. Then she glanced up at him. "She's sending two officers to talk to Nanette Espinoza."

"You don't look happy about that," he noted.

She sighed. "I don't know how much credence they're putting in my ability to read lips. But I know what I saw."

"I believe you." He stroked Bravo again, then reached for Aubrey's hand. Keeping their hands joined, he addressed his dog. "Bravo, this is Aubrey. Aubrey is a friend, Bravo. Friend."

Bravo sniffed their hands for a long moment before his tail wagged back and forth.

"He's a beautiful dog."

"Thank you. We've been home for a few months now, but he's still a highly trained military K9 and can be aggressive at times." Something that came in very handy when tracking terrorists, not so much while walking among the citizens of San Diego. "You need to be careful around him."

"I understand." She smiled as Bravo licked the back of her hand. "Well, I guess it's time for me to head home."

"Bravo and I will escort you, just to be safe."

She nodded and stood. She may have said something, but he couldn't be sure. Not hearing statements and other sounds was extremely frustrating. At first, he'd railed in anger that this had happened to him. Then he pulled himself together and decided to set an example for the rest of his teammates. Kaleb, Hudson, Dallas, Dawson, and Nico hadn't emerged unscathed either. They'd all suffered during that last deployment, barely escaping a dicey situation that had claimed the life of one of their teammates, Jaydon Rampart. His fault, Mason silently admitted, as team leader. It was his job to bring them all home.

A job he'd failed, in more ways than one.

Still, as one of the oldest and active SEAL teams, their retirement had been a foregone conclusion by the time they'd returned stateside.

Even without their various injuries and problems, they would have been forced out.

Being a SEAL was a young man's game. Granted, their experience and expertise had carried them along for a few years longer than most, but he'd always known they were operating on borrowed time. He was forty-two, the oldest member of their team.

And there was no doubt that if they'd have retired earlier, Jaydon would still be alive.

Aubrey touched his arm again. "I live this way."

He knew where she lived, which again made him stalker-like. Yet he hadn't been able to help himself. Frankly, he knew where all the adults who took the sign language class lived, only because he spent a lot of time walking the streets with Bravo rather than sleeping. And deep down, he'd needed to know everything about the people surrounding him in the small classroom. "Okay."

". . . followed me . . ."

He tried to piece together what she'd said. "I'm sorry if I came across as a stalker, but I do a lot of walking at night. It helps me sleep."

She looked at him, and he tipped his head to hear better. "I was wondering why Jose, if that's who it was at the apartment, followed me," she repeated carefully. "He probably doesn't know I can read lips."

"Oh." He wondered if he'd ever get used to being 65 percent deaf. "You're right in that most people don't understand the ability to do that. Although it could be there was something else happening in that apartment. A crime he thought you witnessed."

"I hadn't considered that possibility." She turned right at the next intersection. "That only makes Lucas's disappearance more dire."

"I know." He didn't like the thought of a ten-year-old deaf kid being taken or worse, hurt. Doing nothing chafed, but then again, he had his own issues to deal with. And he wasn't officially a SEAL any longer. "Hopefully, the police will find him."

"I intend to keep praying for Lucas until he's found."

Praying? He shied away from talk of faith and God. When he'd been younger and going through the arduous BUD/S training, he'd prayed for strength and endurance every single day. But over the years, he'd remained focused on training and preparation for each mission.

Until the underwater bomb had exploded too close to him.

They walked without speaking for several long moments. When he saw the small robin's egg blue bungalow that she owned, he instinctively slowed his steps. Oddly enough, for a man who preferred to be alone, unless you counted hanging with his teammates, he'd enjoyed this brief time with Aubrey.

"Thanks for walking me home." She paused on the sidewalk. "See you at class."

"Sure." He gave Bravo the hand signal for sit, and the dog dropped to his haunches. The SEALs used hand signals a lot, which is why he'd decided to learn sign language. He regarded Aubrey for a moment. The interior of her small house was dark, but he didn't like leaving her like this. "I'll wait here until you're safely inside."

As he said the words, his peripheral vision picked up some movement. The small black car slowed; the passenger window lowered. Mason was moving by the time he saw the gun barrel.

"Get down!" He launched himself at Aubrey, knocking her to the ground. Bravo barked wildly as gunfire echoed around them. Mason rolled to the side, instinctively reaching for his Sig Sauer, only to remember he'd left it at home because the school didn't allow firearms.

In a flash, the vehicle disappeared around the corner. Bravo's frenzied barking caused several lights to turn on in the houses on either side of Aubrey's. He figured there were at least two faces pressed against the windows, watching.

Furious at being shot at, he lunged to his feet, then reached down to draw Aubrey upright. "I'm sorry, are you okay? Did I hurt you?"

"Who—was that?" She wheezed, putting a hand to her chest. He'd no doubt hit her hard enough to knock the breath from her lungs.

Good question. Things had happened so fast he hadn't gotten a good look at the shooter or the driver.

Had to be the same guy she'd seen in the apartment. Why? He wasn't sure, but his gut warned him that Aubrey's concern over a missing child had gotten her involved in something very dangerous.

Bravo whined beside him, and he took a moment to check the K9 for signs of injury. Thankfully, the dog seemed fine, but he scowled in the direction the car had disappeared.

That idiot had nearly killed his dog and Aubrey. He'd been vested in this situation based on principle, no kid should be in danger. But now?

This had just gotten very personal.

CHAPTER TWO

She couldn't seem to stop shaking. Her body was sore where Mason had plowed into her, but she barely noticed. Someone had tried to shoot her! Jose? The image of the short, stocky guy in Lucas's apartment flashed in her mind.

Aubrey's breathing quickened as she glanced wildly around at her neighbors' homes. "I—have to call the police!"

"Easy now, slow your breathing." Mason cupped her shoulders in his warm hands. "You're hyperventilating. Try to calm down."

"Calm down? Someone tried to kill me!" This was all so unbelievable. Things like this didn't happen to her. Little dots flashed in front of her eyes, and she began to feel light-headed. She stared into Mason's eyes, doing her best to slow her breathing.

"That's better," he said. "Another deep breath in and out."

She followed his direction, mesmerized by his deep voice. The dizziness faded, the spots disappearing from her vision. She swallowed hard. "Okay, thanks. We still need to call the police."

"Yes, we do." He stared at her for a long moment before releasing her and stepping back. He gestured with his hand, and Bravo came to stand beside him. "We're not staying here, though. They know where you live."

Aubrey could feel herself starting to hyperventilate again. They knew her name and address? She turned to look at the street in front of her house. Would they come back later tonight?

"Come with me," Mason said. "I'll protect you."

She was so far out of her depth of experience that she simply nodded. Going with Mason was easier than trying to come up with another plan.

"Let's go inside so you can pack a bag." Mason glanced at her. "I don't suppose you have a car?"

"I, uh, yes. I have a car." She didn't use it much, preferring to walk to and from the school.

She wondered if she'd ever feel safe walking again.

"Aubrey?" Mason's voice broke into her thoughts. She pulled herself together with an effort and grabbed her keys from her small purse. He gently took the keys from her hand and opened the door for her. "Stay right inside the doorway here for a minute, Bravo and I will clear the place."

She sagged against the wall, her knees threatening to collapse. She subtly rubbed her throbbing tailbone. The pain only reinforced that this entire situation wasn't a nightmare. It was real. All too real.

Her bungalow was small, so it didn't take long for Mason and Bravo to return. "Go on, pack a bag," he said. "Then if it's okay, we'll take your car to my house."

Going to his place should have filled her with apprehension. It didn't. Instead, she was grateful to go with Mason rather than being left alone.

She tossed a couple of clothing items and toiletries into

a small rolling suitcase. When she returned to the living room, she paused. Mason was sitting on the edge of her sofa, his head buried against Bravo's fur. The love he had for his dog shone bright and true.

"Mason? I'm ready." She made sure to speak clearly.

His head snapped up, and he instantly rose to his feet. If he was embarrassed by the display of emotion, he didn't let on. "Good." He came forward, taking the bag from her hand. "Let's get out of here."

Since Mason still had her keys, she waited for him to lock the front door before heading to the garage. She punched in the code, and the door opened, revealing her white Kia sedan.

"I hope you don't mind dog hair in the back seat," he said as he opened the rear passenger door for Bravo. "He sheds."

"Of course not." Dog hair was the least of her worries.

"I'll drive if that's okay." He didn't wait for an answer but opened the passenger door for her. She considered arguing but then realized her hands were still trembling.

Minutes later, they were on the road. Mason drove with relaxed confidence, although she could tell he was hyper-aware of his surroundings. "Thanks for letting me drive, it's easier for me to hold a conversation this way."

She belatedly remembered his right ear was his good one. "It's not a problem. But where do you live? I mean, are you far from the school?"

"About twenty minutes." He glanced at her. "I have a small house, similar to yours."

She nodded, suspecting that owning a home was smart when you had a dog. "I was able to keep my house after my husband died."

"I'm sorry for your loss."

She flushed. "Thanks. It's been many years now, so I'm fine." A sudden thought hit hard. "Um, is your wife or girl-friend going to be upset when I show up?"

"No wife, no girlfriend," he answered easily. "Just me and Bravo."

She was curious about why a good-looking guy like Mason was single, then reminded herself it was none of her business. Easy to imagine that being a SEAL made dating difficult. At thirty-eight, she wasn't looking to jump into another relationship. Her hand instinctively covered her lower abdomen. She'd lost her baby boy ten years ago. A miscarriage that had happened at eighteen weeks, some-thing the doctors had assured her was not common.

If her son had lived, he'd be Lucas's age. Maybe that was part of the reason she'd grown attached to the child. Not that there weren't other boys and girls in her class, but the way Lucas had kept to himself and his quiet and shy demeanor had caused her to draw him out. Then there were the bruises. And the call to CPS.

Her heart squeezed painfully. Now he was gone. Miss-ing, or worse . . .

She wondered what the police had found when they'd gone to the apartment. Had Nanette kept to the script, telling them the boy ran away? Or had the young mother broken down and confessed about what had really happened?

Please, God, grant her the strength to tell the truth!

Bravo placed his head on the center console. His sweet face made her smile.

Mason reached back to scratch the dog behind the ears. "Bravo is a good guard dog. No one will get close while he's around."

"I know. His barking was enough to scare them off." As

she watched, Bravo closed his eyes beneath Mason's touch.

"You didn't get a license plate number, did you?"

"No." She smiled wryly. "I was taken to the dirt by the cornerback, remember?"

He winced. "I'm sorry about that."

"Don't be. You saved my life." Her smile faded as she realized once again how close they'd come to dying today. If not for Mason's quick reflexes, and the dog's mad barking, she suspected the outcome would have been very different. "I'm sorry I dragged you into this mess."

"I'm the stalker who followed you, remember?"

She shuddered thinking about how the night would have ended if he hadn't. "I'm sick over Lucas," she admitted. "He's the true innocent here."

"We have to trust the police will find him."

They entered a neighborhood that was a step up from hers. Mason pulled into the driveway of a white house that appeared larger than hers, despite his comment. "Nice place."

"Thanks." He let the dog out of the back and grabbed her suitcase.

As she followed the man and the dog inside, she found herself reconsidering this idea. What did she really know about Mason Gray? Just because he used to be a Navy SEAL didn't mean he was above reproach. Maybe he'd been dishonorably discharged from the military. Maybe he'd kidnapped Lucas and was there to prevent her from learning the truth. Maybe . . .

"Aubrey, take a deep breath. You're hyperventilating again."

His deep voice broke through her crazy thoughts. She'd never had a panic attack in her life, and now she'd experienced two of them in a matter of minutes.

"I'm fine." She managed a smile. "I'm not normally like this."

"It's been a rough evening. You're entitled to be upset."

She caught a glimpse of a pool through a set of patio doors. It made sense that he was a swimmer, didn't the SEALs call themselves the frogmen?

"Let me show you the guest room." Mason moved down a short hallway. He gestured to one doorway, then another. "This is the bathroom; your room is right next door."

"Thank you." She watched as he set her suitcase on the bed. From their brief walk-through, it appeared the house was meticulously clean. Her husband had always been a slob, but maybe this was some sort of holdover from Mason's time in the military.

It had been a long time since she'd thought of Carter, her husband. The aggressive form of leukemia had taken him so quickly, she'd barely had time to comprehend the magnitude of his diagnosis before he was placed in hospice. She'd suffered her miscarriage a mere three months before Carter had died. The twin losses had been staggering.

"We need to call the police," Mason said. "When that's finished, I'll throw together a couple of grilled cheese sandwiches for dinner."

She wasn't hungry, but she also wasn't quite ready to be alone either. "Okay."

As he led the way back to the kitchen, she took out her phone and stared at it. "It feels wrong to call 911 after the danger is over."

"Call anyway. They may have received calls from your neighbors as well. Oh, and put the call on speaker, they need to know I was a witness."

For the second time in her life, she punched in the numbers. This time, the voice that answered was male.

"This is Aubrey Clark, and I'm calling to report an attempt to kill me outside my home tonight."

"Are you hurt?"

"No, but only because I had help from a friend." Her gaze landed on Mason.

"My name is Mason Gray, and I was a witness to the shooting," he said.

"You need to know I called earlier with a concern about a missing boy named Lucas Espinoza," Aubrey quickly added. "I believe this recent gunfire is a direct result of that crime because the man inside the apartment followed me. Mr. Gray helped me get away."

"Officers have been dispatched to the scene." The dispatcher rattled off her address.

"That is correct, only I didn't stay at my house," she told him. "I'm with Mason."

"I'll be happy to give you my address," Mason added.

"Hold on, it will be easier if I have Detective Russo call you. He'll want to speak with you about the sequence of events."

"That's fine." She listened as he verified her phone number. "Thank you." She disconnected from the call and sat back in her seat. "I have a feeling the detective will want to come out here, sorry about that."

"It's what I expected." Mason turned away and busied himself at the stove.

Aubrey took a deep breath and let it out slowly. It seemed as if this would be a very long night.

HE'D EXPECTED to feel crowded and uncomfortable with Aubrey invading his personal space, but he didn't. At least, not yet. Having given his life to the SEALs, he could count on one hand how many female guests had visited him.

Not because there hadn't been plenty of women interested, especially in those early years. Since SEALs trained in Coronado, which was part of the San Diego area, there were plenty of women who frequented the popular bars and pubs where the guys tended to hang out. Especially McP's, an Irish pub where most of the young single guys hung out on a regular basis.

But it hadn't taken long for him to lose interest in that sort of lifestyle. Most women idolized the SEALs without any understanding of how difficult it was to be in a relationship with a guy who left the country with less than five minutes notice and couldn't talk about where they'd been or what they'd done. The SEAL life was far from glamorous. He'd seen his fair share of hasty marriages and even quicker divorces.

Breakups like that tended to wreck a guy's concentration, which was not a good thing in the middle of a dicey op with tangos coming at you from all sides.

Bravo stretched out on the floor near Aubrey's chair as if understanding his job was to keep her safe. The grilled cheese sandwiches didn't take long. He slid a plate over to her, then sat beside her.

"Thank you." He sat to her left so he could hear her better. He'd learned a fair amount of sign language in the past ten weeks, but deep down, he was hoping he wouldn't need it for the long haul.

Not that there had been any improvement in his hearing over that same time frame. The doc had warned him it may be permanent. Not only that, but his right ear could potentially get worse over time too.

He was so preoccupied with his thoughts, he realized Aubrey had bowed her head to silently pray over their food. He felt guilty having already taken a bite.

"Mason?" He glanced up from his sandwich. "How long do you think I need to stay here?"

"Until they catch the guy who shot at us."

"But what if they don't catch him?" She'd only eaten half her sandwich; the events from the evening seemed to be weighing her down. "I can't just stay here indefinitely. Besides, I want to help find Lucas."

"Let's wait to see what the detective has to say." He finished his first sandwich and started on his second. He understood her desire to find the child; he didn't like knowing the kid was in danger either. Yet, he was concerned about her safety. Aubrey was his primary concern.

He considered calling a couple of the guys for help. They'd all retired from the team at the same time and had pretty much stayed in the same area. At least, initially. He hadn't spoken to any of them in several weeks. Not since he'd introduced them to Lillian, the woman who rescued dogs and trained them to be K9 specialists. Each of the guys had adopted a dog with different strengths and training. He'd figured they'd need time to adjust to their new lives. The same way he'd had to.

"Mason?" He glanced sharply at Aubrey. She flushed and gestured toward the living room. "I think the detective is here."

He belatedly realized Bravo was standing and staring intently at the front door. Man, he needed to get his head screwed on straight. If the bad guys had come to finish the job, they'd all end up dead.

He rose and crossed over to peer through the front

window. When he saw the two men wearing ill-fitting suits holding up gold badges, he gave Bravo the signal for sit and stay before opening the door.

"Mr. Gray?" The taller, younger of the two men held up his gold shield. "I'm Detective Russo. This is my partner, Detective Lee."

He couldn't remember ever being addressed as Mr. Gray. He'd always been addressed by his rank, but this was the civilian life that he needed to get used to. He nodded and stepped back. "Come in. Aubrey Clark is in the kitchen."

The two men stepped over the threshold, then stopped abruptly when they saw Bravo. The dog was too well trained to growl, but the animal was on high alert.

"Call off your dog," Lee said.

Mason arched a brow. "He's not doing anything."

The older man flushed and glanced at Russo. "We'd feel better if he was kenneled."

"I wouldn't." Mason was not about to kennel his dog. "Bravo is a well-trained Navy SEAL K9. He won't attack unless I give the command."

"A SEAL, huh?" Russo looked impressed.

"Retired SEAL," he corrected himself. He would always consider himself a SEAL, even though he was formally discharged from service. "This way, please." He led the way into the kitchen. Aubrey slowly rose to her feet. "Aubrey, Detectives Russo and Lee."

She nodded. "Thanks for coming."

"Please have a seat." Mason quickly finished his second sandwich and took both plates to the counter. Bravo stayed close to his side.

"Ms. Clark, please tell us what happened outside your house this evening," Russo said.

He tamped down a flash of impatience. "It might be better if she starts at the beginning."

Now Lee looked annoyed. "It's important to hear about the alleged gunfire," he shot back.

"Please, let me explain," Aubrey said, taking a mediator role. "I'm a teacher at the Stanley School for the Deaf. One of my students, a ten-year-old named Lucas, came to class on Monday with bruises on his arms. When I asked about them, he claimed he fell off his bike, but the bruises looked to me like they were done by a hand grabbing him. I filed report with Child Protective Services, but then Lucas didn't show up for school on Tuesday or today."

Both detectives were paying attention now. "Go on," Russo encouraged.

"I know where Lucas lives because his mother didn't know sign language, and I wanted to discuss the possibility of her taking my free adult classes. I went there tonight hoping to talk to her again when I saw a man in the apartment. He looked angry, and when he turned, I read his lips through the window. He said, 'You'll tell the police he ran away.'" Aubrey swallowed hard. "Then he also said, 'Do you want to disappear too?'"

"You're sure about that?" Lee asked, doubt clear in his gaze.

"I'm positive. I was born deaf and learned to read lips. I was blessed to receive a cochlear implant seven years ago and have worked hard to improve my speech." She waved a hand. "I know what I saw. Besides, when the man in the apartment saw me, he instantly left the building to come after me. I ran away. Thankfully, Mason and Bravo were nearby. Together, we escaped and walked the rest of the way to my house. But as we arrived, the dark car came down the street, and that's when shots were fired at us."

"It was a black Chevy," Mason added. "The minute I saw the gun, I tackled Ms. Clark to the ground. Bravo barked like crazy, which may have helped keep us safe, as the car sped off. Unfortunately, neither one of us was able to get a license plate number."

The two detectives glanced at each other and nodded. "That story is consistent with what we heard from several witnesses in your neighborhood," Russo agreed. "Although we weren't aware of the fact that you'd gone to an apartment to find a missing boy."

Mason had to refrain from pointing out that was why it was important for Aubrey to start her story at the beginning. "She made a 911 call about the child and gave her statement about what she saw through the window of what the man said."

"We'll follow up with the precinct to get the details on that," Russo said. "Can you give me the address?"

Aubrey did so. "It's in East Village."

"Great," Lee muttered. "Those neighbors won't be nearly as accommodating."

Mason understood what he meant. The city was putting a lot of effort into renovating East Village, especially around Petco Park, but the crime rate was still far too high. Something that would need to change if the city wanted to attract a family-friendly atmosphere along with better paying jobs.

"What is the boy's full name?" Russo asked.

"Lucas Espinoza, I'm afraid I don't know his middle name. His mother is Nanette Espinoza, and the last I heard, she had a boyfriend named Jose living with them." Aubrey frowned. "I tried to get Lucas to tell me if Jose hurt him, but he insisted he fell off his bike."

"You don't have a last name for this Jose?" Lee asked.

"No. But I'm sure Nanette will give it to you. I know she cares about Lucas."

Aubrey's faith in humanity was admirable, but Mason wasn't convinced. Granted, he'd seen the worst side of people, along with the awful things they did to each other. For her sake, he hoped she was right.

"I'll call the precinct, see if an officer has gone out to the apartment yet." Russo rose and moved into the other room to use his phone.

"What do you mean? Wouldn't they have sent someone right away?" Aubrey was clearly upset by the detective's statement.

"That depends on what else might be going on," Lee said with a shrug.

Mason put a calming hand on Aubrey's arm. "We just thought a missing child would be considered a high priority."

"It is," Lee said quickly. "Although, on the other hand, we only have your word for what you think the guy said. Frankly, I'm not sure the whole lipreading thing will stand up in court."

"Why not?" Aubrey asked hotly. She shook off Mason's hand and leaned toward the older detective. "I know what I saw. How do you think deaf people navigate the world, huh? Your average person doesn't know sign language, so we're forced to learn to lip-read."

Lee held up his hands. "Okay, okay. Maybe I'm wrong and it will stand up in court."

"Why do you think the man in the apartment bothered to chase after Ms. Clark?" Mason kept his gaze on the detective. "Logically, she wouldn't be a threat standing outside in the cold when the windows are closed. No way to hear a conversation that way. Unless Lucas's mother mentioned the possibility of Ms. Clark being able to read lips. Then it makes perfect sense why he came after her with a gun."

"Exactly," Aubrey agreed. "That's the only logical explanation."

Lee slowly nodded. "I see your point."

Mason had more faith in Russo than this guy. After a few minutes, Russo returned to the kitchen, his expression serious.

"I spoke to the officer who went to the apartment. Nanette Espinoza did tell them her son ran away. But then she broke down crying and refused to talk to them anymore. Apparently, she had a bruise on her cheek."

"I knew Jose grabbed Lucas's arm," Aubrey said harshly. "He may have even hit the boy someplace where I couldn't see the bruises."

"There was no sign of a man being there either," Russo continued. "Nanette claimed she lived there alone with her son."

Mason stared at him. "She denied knowing a man named Jose?"

"Yes. Claimed she wasn't seeing anyone." Russo paused, then added, "Our officers found a black Chevy that was reported stolen abandoned near the park. Could be the car used by the shooter. We'll have crime scene techs check for prints, but I wouldn't get your hopes up. They seem to think the vehicle was wiped down."

He blew out a breath. "So, basically, you have nothing."

The two detectives shared a glance. "Yeah, but we'll keep looking into it."

As he walked them to the door, Mason knew they'd try their best, but he didn't have a whole lot of faith in their ability to get to the bottom of this.

Which left Aubrey in the bull's-eye of danger.

CHAPTER THREE

Aubrey was shocked to learn Nanette lied to the police about her boyfriend. She understood the poor woman was probably scared out of her mind, the bruise on her cheek was likely a warning to keep quiet, but Lucas was her son.

What mother didn't do whatever possible to protect her son?

"Aubrey? Are you okay?"

"No. I want to shake Nanette until she tells the truth about what happened to Lucas." She slowly shook her head. "I feel so helpless. If I had any idea where to start looking, I'd search for him myself."

"I know you would." Mason rested his hand on her shoulder. "But let's focus on keeping you safe."

She scowled. "Our focus should be on finding a scared, vulnerable, deaf ten-year-old boy."

Mason pulled the chair out so that he was facing her. "Did Jose have any tattoos or other identifying marks? Is it possible he has gang connections? San Diego is pretty far from LA, but our city is not immune as Mexican drug cartels are spreading their tentacles across the southern part of the state."

"Maybe." Closing her eyes, she brought the image of the guy in the apartment to the forefront of her mind. "There might have been a tattoo on his neck, but I can't say for sure what the design was. I was paying more attention to reading his lips to understand what he was saying."

"A tattoo on his neck is a good start." Mason's tone was encouraging. "Did Lucas say anything specific about Jose?"

"When I asked him directly about Jose, he denied the man had caused his bruises, even though they were clearly fingerprints that had been dug into his skin." She thought back to their sign language conversation. "Lucas seemed afraid of Jose, at least that's the impression I had. But, of course, he didn't say that."

"How long has Jose been in the picture?"

That was easy. "Three weeks. I know for sure because Nanette stopped attending my adult class, and when I went to her apartment to talk to her, she told me she had a new boyfriend and she was working later hours, so she couldn't continue to take my classes. I tried to explain how important it was for Lucas to have someone to speak sign language with, but she wouldn't change her mind." And now the child was gone. The role she'd inadvertently played in his disappearance haunted her.

"You didn't meet Jose when you went to the apartment?"

She shook her head. "I wasn't invited to go inside, which looking back seems a bit strange. Nanette and I only spoke briefly at the door."

Bravo rested his chin on Mason's knee. He stroked his dog's fur with a gentleness that reassured her that he was a good man. The way he'd saved her life, twice in a matter of an hour, spoke volumes too.

Still, being in his personal space had her on edge. She hadn't been this close to a man in ten years. Since her husband's death, months after delivering their stillborn son, she'd kept to herself. Aubrey hadn't been interested in dating, especially in those early years. And now it was almost too late since some of the men her age seemed to prefer younger women.

Considering her biological clock was on its downward spiral, she could understand. A man looking to start a family wasn't going to date a thirty-eight-going-on-thirty-nine-year-old woman. Something that hadn't bothered her at all, until recently.

So why was she so keenly aware of Mason Gray? If she were honest, she'd admit she'd found him attractive the first time she'd met him over two months ago, when he'd attended his first sign language class. She wasn't the only one, several of the younger women had been engrossed by him too. Mason had broad shoulders and dark hair cut military short with just a hint of gray at his temples. And a pair of piercing blue eyes. He had a tattoo on his upper bicep, but his shirt sleeve partially covered it so that she wasn't sure what it was. He'd always been quiet and polite. She'd been drawn to him, even then.

Too bad the feeling was not mutual. He'd barely noticed her as a woman, his concentration focused on learning what he needed to know. *Which is how it should be,* she reminded herself sternly. She was a teacher, and dating a student, even an adult student, would be inappropriate.

"Maybe you should get some rest." Mason's deep voice pulled her from her thoughts. "It's been a long day."

"Yes, it sure has." She forced herself to stand. "I plan to

leave here about seven thirty for school. Thanks again for everything."

"Wait." He shot to his feet and grasped her wrist; the warmth of his fingers sent a prickly tingle shooting up her arm. Bravo jumped to his feet too, glancing between them as if trying to figure out what was going on. "I don't think going to school tomorrow is a good idea. Jose and his buddy know you're a teacher there."

"I have to. My kids are depending on me." She tried to smile. "Maybe Lucas will show up and prove he's fine."

Mason's blue eyes bored into hers. "You don't really believe that."

She lifted her chin. "I believe in God and the power of prayer. I intend to pray for Lucas's safe return." She gently pulled out of his grasp. "Good night, Mason." Then she smiled at the dog. "Good night, Bravo."

"Good night." Mason stepped back to allow her to step past him.

She pulled her pajamas and toothbrush from her suitcase and ducked into the bathroom. Her pajamas were very modest, but she still felt uncomfortable prancing around in them in front of Mason. Ridiculous, really, as he'd been nothing but a gentleman.

When she finished in the bathroom, she stood for a moment feeling self-conscious. She heard a door open and close. Mason had likely taken Bravo outside. Feeling foolish, she peeked out of the bathroom door. When she found the hallway empty, she gratefully hurried back to the guest room.

Despite her sore muscles and bone-deep exhaustion, sleep didn't come easily. Being in a strange bed didn't help, although it was very comfortable. No, the biggest problem was that the events of the evening kept rolling through her mind.

She put all her faith into her prayers. Begging the Lord to protect Lucas while guiding the boy home.

Aubrey realized she must have fallen asleep because she woke with a start. Had she heard a noise? It took a second to remember she was in Mason's house, not hers.

Picking up her phone attached to its charger, she noted the time was six o'clock. She had to smile at how she woke up at the same time each day. Listening intently, she decided the sound she'd heard was either Mason taking care of Bravo or a figment of her wild imagination.

She tiptoed to the bathroom carrying her clothes and toiletries. After a quick shower, she changed and let her long hair air-dry. When she emerged from the bathroom, the enticing scent of coffee and bacon made her stomach rumble.

After making the bed, she joined Mason and Bravo in the kitchen. She was surprised to see Mason was dressed in black slacks and a light blue long-sleeved shirt.

She cleared her throat loudly. "Good morning, Mason."

He looked over at her and smiled. He was so attractive. She had the most ridiculous urge to throw herself into his arms. "Good morning. I hope you're hungry."

"You don't have to cook for me," she protested.

"I have to cook for myself anyway." He gestured toward the coffeepot. "Help yourself."

She did, thankful for the kick of caffeine. "You look dressed up, are you going somewhere today?"

"Yeah, to your classroom." He barely glanced at her as he continued making scrambled eggs. The bacon was already finished.

"What?" She stared, her coffee cup halfway to her mouth. "Why?"

He didn't answer. She belatedly realized she'd moved to his left side and quickly went over to stand at his right. "Mason, why are you coming with me today?"

"I plan to be there in case Jose and the shooter show up." His expression was serious. "Your kids could be in danger too."

She sucked in a harsh breath. That possibility hadn't occurred to her. "They wouldn't try something in the middle of the day," she protested.

"Hopefully not. But we need to plan for the worst-case scenario." He filled two plates with scrambled eggs, added two strips of bacon to each, and handed one to her. "I called one of my Navy SEAL teammates last night. Kaleb is hoping to head down later today."

"You really think I'm putting the kids in danger?" She carried her plate to the table and sat down.

"I don't know," he admitted. "As you say, trying something during the day with lots of witnesses wouldn't be smart. But it's best to be prepared."

She stared down at her plate, her earlier appetite having vanished. Indecision tore at her. Substitute teachers were nearly impossible to find for deaf students. Having a teacher who didn't know sign language was no help to them at all. Yet she didn't want to put them in danger either.

Today was Thursday. Two days of school left in the week.

Aubrey sighed and caved. "Okay, fine. I'll call in sick to school to keep the kids safe. I'll spend the day driving around to look for Lucas."

He narrowed his gaze. "And where exactly do you plan to search?"

It was a good question. "His neighborhood. Maybe someone has seen him or knows something."

"I'll go with you." Mason's tone didn't invite an argument.

"Fine with me." She wasn't keen on facing men with guns alone anyway. Picking up her fork, she forced herself to eat. She'd need strength and courage to find Lucas.

Along with a whole lot of faith.

———

WITH BRAVO STRETCHED out at his feet, Mason managed to refrain from eating until Aubrey said grace. He deduced she'd said the prayer out loud for his benefit. The relief of having convinced Aubrey not to go to school had quickly evaporated when she'd announced her plan to look for Lucas herself.

It was a job for law enforcement, not a schoolteacher. Yet he couldn't deny sharing her desire to find the boy. A deaf kid was twice as vulnerable.

Last night, when he'd called Kaleb, it was his buddy's idea to use Bravo's keen nose to help search for the kid. It wasn't a half-bad plan. Yet he didn't have anything to use as a scent cue for his partner.

Then he thought about Aubrey's classroom. "Does Lucas have anything at school, like a jacket or sweatshirt? Maybe a pair of boots?"

She frowned. "I think he left a sweatshirt on a hook outside the classroom. I remember thinking I would take it with me to the apartment last night, but I forgot."

He glanced at his watch. "We need to get over there to grab it."

"Why?" Her expression was baffled.

"Bravo is a trained scent tracker. The sweatshirt can be used as a scent source for him to follow."

Her hazel eyes widened with excitement. "Really? Then let's go!"

"Hold on, finish your breakfast first." He glanced down at Bravo, then back at Aubrey. "Scent tracking isn't as easy as they make it seem on TV. Bravo is very talented, but that doesn't mean this will be like following bread crumbs. There will be millions of different scents for him to sift through, especially here in the city where there are so many people. It's worth a try, but I don't want you to get your hopes up that this will work."

The light dimmed from her hazel gaze, but she nodded. "I understand. Honestly, Mason, it's better than sitting around doing nothing. I need to find him. Even . . ." Her voice trailed off, and she swallowed hard.

He knew what she was about to say. Even if that meant finding out the boy was dead.

They finished their breakfast, and Aubrey insisted on helping with the dishes. Having her so close was driving him nuts. Not because he didn't like her. But because he did. Too much.

He glanced at his phone, wishing Kaleb would text to let him know how soon he'd arrive.

Calling his buddy had served two purposes. Not only would Kaleb and his recently acquired female pit bull–lab mix, Sierra, assist in searching for Lucas, but the guy would also serve as a buffer between him and Aubrey.

Frankly, he was tempted to call up his entire team. The more the merrier. But he managed to refrain.

Pathetic that he was allowing a beautiful woman to get under his skin. With nerves of steel, he'd hunted down more terrorists and performed more hairy rescue missions than any other SEAL team, yet he couldn't seem to ignore Aubrey.

Maybe he'd lost more than half his mind, along with 65 percent of his hearing, on that last mission.

"You might want to change into jeans," he said when the kitchen was clean. "You'll blend in better with the crowd in Lucas's neighborhood."

"What about you?" She gestured to his clothes.

"I'm going to change too. And you need to know I'm carrying a gun as well."

Her eyes widened. "A gun? Why on earth do you have a gun?"

No point in letting her know that after serving the military for twenty-two years, he felt naked without it. "For safety." Without waiting for a response, he turned and headed into his room.

He returned a few minutes later. After holstering his Sig Sauer on his belt, he used a hand signal to call Bravo over. The K9 quickly emerged from beneath the kitchen table, sitting at his feet. Mason clicked the leash to his collar. Bravo straightened, his dark eyes alert, clearly knowing it was time to work.

Aubrey joined him a short time later, and he found her even more attractive in casual clothes. He gave himself a mental shake. *Get over it,* he told himself sternly.

"We'll take my SUV, there's a dog crate for Bravo." He handed her the keys to her Kia. "Move your car for me so I can pull mine out of the garage."

They jockeyed vehicles until Aubrey's white sedan was in the garage. Then she jumped into the passenger seat of his SUV. "I made the call to the school that I wouldn't be in, so I hope we don't run into anyone when we pick up the sweatshirt."

"Understood." He wasn't worried, but then again, it wasn't his job on the line.

The trip to the Stanley School for the Deaf didn't take long. He decided to leave Bravo in the SUV, it was equipped with an automatic temperature sensor that would start the engine if it grew too warm or too cold. Besides, they wouldn't be gone for long.

Aubrey led the way inside to her classroom. He knew where it was located because he'd been there several times when he'd arrived early for the adult sign language class. He didn't bother to hide his gun, even though weapons were clearly not allowed. She stopped in the hallway and pointed to a badly stained and holey sweatshirt hanging on a hook. "That one belongs to Lucas."

He'd come prepared with a plastic bag. Using the tips of his fingers, he lifted the garment up and dropped it inside. "Thanks, this should work really well."

"I have something to get from inside the classroom." She unlocked the door and went inside, returning less than thirty seconds later. In her hand, he saw a small photograph.

"That's Lucas?"

"Yes." She showed him the small square photo glued to the inside of a red paper apple. "It was taken at the beginning of the year."

"Good idea to grab it." He took a moment to commit the boy's features to memory. Then he quickly escorted Aubrey from the building.

"Next stop, Lucas's apartment," she said once they were settled inside the SUV.

"Yeah." He was a little apprehensive about going there, but it was the most likely spot for Bravo to pick up the boy's scent.

At least this time, he was armed with both his Sig Sauer

and an Ontario MK 3 knife with a 6-inch steel blade. Both weapons were standard issue for all SEALs. He also had the added benefit of Bravo's sharp teeth, which could do just as much damage.

He drove toward Lucas's apartment, keeping a keen gaze out for any sign of danger. Kaleb had promised to hit the road first thing, so he figured his buddy would get there sooner than later.

"I hope we find Jose," Aubrey said.

He shot her a glance. "If we do, we'll call the police." He wasn't about to put Aubrey in danger or step on the local law enforcement's toes. As retired military, he had absolutely no jurisdiction here.

"He knows where Lucas is," she said grimly. "I know he does."

She was probably right. Seeing a rare parking space, he instantly pulled over. They were within walking distance of the apartment building. He wished Aubrey would stay in the car. "Stay here while Bravo and I scope the place out."

"No, I'm coming with you." She pushed open her door. "Lucas is my student. He's in trouble because of me. And if we do happen to find him, he'll know me and feel safe enough to come with us."

He swallowed a surge of frustration and nodded. He grabbed the bag containing the sweatshirt, then climbed from the car. After letting Bravo out of the back crate area, he offered the scent bag to his partner.

"This is Lucas. Seek!"

Bravo took a long sniff, then lifted his snout to the air, searching for a scent cone. Bravo was good, but he hadn't been kidding about the infinite number of scents teeming about the city. Zeroing in on Lucas's scent, especially if it had been a couple of days since the boy had been there, would not be easy.

Bravo moved forward, his nose still in the air. Mason sensed Aubrey's impatience but lifted a hand to keep her quiet. Not that Bravo needed silence to do his job, but he couldn't watch the dog and keep an eye on her at the same time.

Since he was left-handed and may need to draw his weapon, Bravo was on his right, which left Aubrey on his left. Having his deaf ear toward her made it difficult to hear.

They quickly covered the three blocks to the two-story apartment building. Bravo picked up his pace, his nose working. The sunlight meant the windows of the apartment were opaque, so he couldn't see inside from a distance. When the dog sat near the front door of the apartment building, he barked to let Mason know he'd found Lucas's scent.

"Good boy, Bravo. Good boy!" He praised his K9 and gave him a rub. Bravo's tail whipped back and forth with excitement at a job well done. But their task was far from over. He'd hoped the apartment would be a good starting point, and that instinct had proven correct.

Aubrey put her hand on his arm. He turned to look at her. "I didn't see anyone inside the apartment, did you?"

"No." He glanced around and then moved back to the corner apartment. Up close, he cupped his hands around his face. He could see the living space, but other than the threadbare furniture and scattered beer cans, there was no sign of the occupants.

"Let's keep working with Bravo." He offered the scent bag again and repeated the command. "Seek! Seek Lucas!"

The dog took another long sniff, then headed back toward the apartment building. Mason didn't reward him for alerting at the same spot, and soon the dog continued moving along the side of the street.

If the kid had been shoved into a car, this would likely be a short search. But Bravo continued, lifting his nose to the air following some thread of a scent that only an expert tracker could identify.

Aubrey said something that he missed. He glanced over, and she repeated herself. "He's impressive."

"Yeah, he is." Bravo had saved his butt and that of his team members more than once.

The K9 slowed and sniffed near a small café. When the dog alerted there, he once again offered praise.

"You think Lucas is inside?" Aubrey asked with a frown. "Even though it doesn't open until eight thirty?"

"No, but he might have been here recently." He eyed the café. "Where did Nanette work?"

Aubrey shook her head. "I have no idea. She never mentioned it."

He stood and looked around. The kid could have come this way before or after school, maybe waited around the area until his mother would be home from her job.

Or maybe he had stayed here to avoid going home at all.

A kid came whizzing toward them on a skateboard. He looked to be about Lucas's age, maybe a year or two older. The kid tried to scoot around them, but Mason quickly grabbed the boy's arm, pulling him to a stop.

"Hey, whattaya doin'?" The kid glared at him as he pretty much fell off the board.

"I need to find Lucas Espinoza. Do you know where he is?"

"I don't know nuthin'," the kid said with a pout.

Aubrey held up Lucas's school picture. "This boy is missing. We need to find him."

The kid scowled. "How should I know? Dude is deaf and dumb."

"And how do you know that?" Mason asked. Good thing the kid wasn't too bright. "You must know him if you know he's deaf."

"I mighta seen him around." The kid shrugged, then stared up at him shrewdly. "Is there a reward for finding him?"

"Shouldn't you be in school?" Aubrey demanded.

The kid looked defiant. "It's a teacher's day off."

"No, it's not," Aubrey said. "Now if you don't want us to call the police to have you arrested for truancy, then I suggest you tell us where Lucas is."

"You can't get arrested for not going to school," he protested.

Mason tightened his grip on the kid's arm. "Yeah, you can. Tell you what, if your information helps us find the boy, I'll give you that reward. But you need to tell us where and when you last saw him."

"Ow, you're hurtin' me." Mason ignored his whining. "Okay, look, the kid is a dummy, right? But I've seen him around. He comes here to meet his mom after school. Pretty sure I saw him a couple of days ago."

"Does his mother work here at the café?" Aubrey asked.

The kid snorted. "Yeah, if you call selling yourself for sex workin'."

Aubrey paled at the implication Nanette was a prostitute. Mason wasn't satisfied. "Be more specific. How many days ago did you see him?"

The kid thought about it. "Tuesday?"

"Are you asking me or telling me?"

"I dunno! I think it was Tuesday." He nodded to himself. "The kid was crying, and she was moving her hands around like this." He waved his hands back and forth.

"She was using sign language?" Aubrey pressed.

"Oh, yeah." The kid looked surprised. "That musta been it."

"What's your name?" Mason asked.

"Denny Highland."

"Thanks. We appreciate your help." This kid could not afford to miss school, he needed all the help he could get. But Mason was glad to have a lead, even a flimsy one. "Let's keep going," he said to Aubrey.

"What about my reward?" Denny demanded.

He was about to give the kid ten bucks when he saw a dark gray car moving slowly down the street. There was something about it that reminded him of the black car the night before. "Get down!" He shoved Denny to the ground and pulled his weapon. Bravo let out several staccato barks as the passenger window began to lower.

The glimpse of a gun barrel was all he needed. He shot the front engine. The vehicle swerved under the impact. The window rolled up, and the vehicle careened around the corner, disappearing out of sight.

CHAPTER FOUR

Aubrey had dropped to the ground upon Mason's shout. She'd noticed the car, too, but hadn't anticipated that Jose would try the same thing as last night. Despite her revulsion for guns, she was glad Mason had been armed.

"Are you okay?" She grasped Denny's arm, raking her gaze over the boy. "You're not hurt?"

"I'm fine." Denny's expression was one of grim acceptance as if he'd seen too much violence already in his short life. His gaze was sharpened on Mason. "Why did you shoot at the car engine?"

"My goal wasn't to hurt anyone," Mason spoke in a clipped tone. "We need information on Lucas's whereabouts, and dead men don't talk."

Denny hiked a brow. "That deaf kid is in real trouble, huh?"

"Yeah. Big-time trouble," Mason agreed.

Denny glanced back at the direction the car had taken. "You got some mean dudes gunning for you."

"Did you recognize the car?" Aubrey asked. "Do you know who was driving it?"

"Nah." Denny shook his head. "I'll tell you if I did."

Much of the kid's earlier bravado had disappeared in the face of danger. She hoped that his talking to her and Mason didn't cause trouble for him.

"Denny, do you have a phone?" Mason asked.

"Yeah, just a cheap one." The kid pulled it from his pocket. Mason took the phone and put his phone number in.

"This is my number. If you see Lucas, will you please call me?" Mason handed the kid his phone back along with a twenty-dollar bill from his pocket. "Get yourself something to eat. And be careful. You don't want to attract the bad dude's attention."

"Thanks, man." Denny stepped over to his skateboard, which had rolled away. Minutes later, the kid was gliding out of sight.

"He's not going to be hurt by those men, is he?" she asked. Bad enough she'd gotten Lucas in trouble, she didn't want to be responsible for hurting another young boy.

Mason's expression was grim. "I hope not. It's you they want, not some kid on a skateboard, but these guys don't seem to be very discriminating about where they fire their weapons either. Taking a shot in broad daylight is a big risk, even here in East Village."

"We need to report this incident to Detectives Russo and Lee." She sighed and shook her head. "What are the chances that car was stolen too?"

"The police might find it faster considering I fired a round into it. I would have given chase, but I didn't want to leave you and Denny unprotected."

"We had Bravo," she said with a weak smile, appreciating how the K9 had alerted them to the possible danger.

Mason had his phone out and was scrolling through his

contacts. She listened as he left a message for Detective Russo about another attempt to shoot them along with a brief description of the car, including the round he'd fired into the engine.

"Hopefully, he'll call us back soon." Mason drew Bravo closer and knelt beside the dog, giving him all kinds of praise for being a good boy.

"Should we head back to your place?" She couldn't stop glancing around, worried the driver and the shooter would come back. Maybe this hadn't been such a great idea.

"Let's go just a little farther." He offered the scent bag to Bravo. "Seek Lucas!"

Aubrey was impressed with the dog's ability to track the boy's scent. Denny had confirmed Lucas had been outside the building two days ago. Although Denny's claim that Nanette was a prostitute concerned her. She didn't want to believe that to be true. What did a kid like Denny know about that sort of lifestyle?

Probably more than she cared to admit.

Mason took her hand and tugged her forward. Her nerves were on edge, but she told herself to get over it. Finding Lucas was important. And maybe now that Jose knew Mason was armed, he wouldn't be so quick to try again.

Maybe. She swallowed hard and prayed.

Please, Lord, keep us safe in Your care and guide us to Lucas. Amen.

Bravo's nose must have locked on the boy's scent because he quickened his pace. Mason's stride lengthened, and she walked faster to keep up. They walked for a good fifteen minutes when the dog abruptly sat next to a bus stop bench and let out a short bark.

"Good boy, Bravo," Mason praised. He gave the dog a rub. "Good boy."

"A bus stop?" She tried not to let her keen disappointment show. "Not as helpful as I'd hoped. From this location, Lucas could have been taken anywhere."

"Lucas may have just sat here to rest," Mason pointed out. "We know he walked all around the city to get where he wanted to go. Don't give up hope yet. Let's give Bravo's nose another try."

"Okay." She was ashamed of her poor attitude. Normally, she prided herself on being optimistic. Something she found difficult in the face of Lucas's disappearance. Her concern for the boy's welfare weighed heavily on her shoulders.

She tried to lean on God's strength and the power of prayer.

Bravo went back on the scent trail. His nose in the air, he sniffed for several minutes before moving down the street in a perpendicular direction from the bus stop. They went several blocks at a brisk and steady pace. Hope flickered in her heart when she spied the well-known restaurant on the corner.

"Mason!" she shouted loud enough for him to hear as she stopped in front of the window. She gestured to the place. "Check this out."

"What is it?" Mason frowned at her, then glanced at Bravo, who had dropped to his haunches in front of the restaurant doorway and let out a short bark. That was the signal that he'd found Lucas's scent. "Do you see him? Is he inside?"

"No, but I recognize the uniform the servers are wearing." She gestured to the woman placing breakfast meals on the table. "I forgot about it until now, but I've seen Nanette wearing the exact same uniform a few weeks ago. I believe she came to one of my adult sign language classes straight from work."

Mason gazed through the window, his expression thoughtful. "I vaguely remember that day. I considered following her home but decided to follow the other young woman, Margie Campbell, who'd come to the same class instead."

She gaped. "You followed my students to their homes after class?"

"It's not as creepy as it sounds," he protested, his cheeks flushing red. "I don't sleep much, and I like to know who I'm dealing with."

"News flash, it is as creepy as it sounds," she said firmly. "Nobody follows innocent people home to make sure they aren't a serial killer."

He stared at her, then blew out a breath. "I didn't say I considered any of them to be serial killers. Just that I wanted to know who these classmates were and what types of lives they lived. You're making it sound like a much bigger deal than it is."

Paranoid much? Then again, maybe this was something all Navy SEALs did on a regular basis. Since she'd never known one on a personal level, how could she say for sure? She decided to let that weird trait pass. "Did you follow Nanette home a different night?" She frowned. "I think she only attended four classes."

"No, I didn't get the chance. She stopped coming before I could to that." He shrugged. "Look, I know this probably sounds crazy, but I've been hardwired to expect the worst every single day of my life. I'm also accustomed to knowing every single minute detail of the people I'm tracking." He looked away and shrugged. "I guess it's been difficult to let go of my military training and experience."

She touched his arm to draw his gaze. "Okay, I can understand that." Aubrey could only imagine the world in which he'd lived for so long. "You still need to know that normal people don't follow other people around as a way to decide if they're trustworthy."

"I never claimed to be normal." Mason jutted his chin toward the restaurant. "Let's go inside and ask if Nanette is working."

"I'll go." She put a restraining hand on his arm, glancing down at Bravo. "I don't think they'll allow a dog inside, even one as pretty and talented as Bravo."

Mason frowned, then nodded. "Stay where I can see you."

After the two recent attempts to kill her, she couldn't accuse him of being overprotective. Honestly, she was deeply grateful Mason was helping her at all, weird paranoia and all. She opened the door and walked in.

The hostess greeted her with a smile. "Table for one?"

"Maybe, but I'm hoping to get a table by my friend Nanette Espinoza. Is she working today? Or was she here yesterday and I have my days goofed up?"

"No, she's not working today." The hostess's smile dimmed. "I believe she's off for the rest of the week."

"Oh no, did something happen?" Aubrey put a hand over her heart. "I hope there isn't trouble with her son, Lucas. He's such a sweet boy."

"I'm sorry, I really can't discuss my fellow employee's personal life." The words were smooth, but the hostess looked around nervously as if worried about someone overhearing their conversation. "We have plenty of excellent servers on duty today. Are you interested in being seated?"

"No, thanks anyway. If you see Nanette, please tell her Aubrey says hi." She turned away, her thoughts whirling.

The good news was that Nanette having a server job at the restaurant made it less likely she was working as a prostitute. But Lucas's mother was also not working today or the rest of the week. Why? Because of her son going missing?

"Well?" Mason drew her from the doorway and over to the side of the building, away from the windows. "What did she say?"

"It seems Nanette isn't working today or the rest of the week, but the hostess wouldn't give me any more information than that. Not even if Nanette was working yesterday. Or if Lucas is the reason for her absence." She sighed. "I'm afraid I didn't learn much, other than Nanette isn't a prostitute."

"To be fair, we don't know that for sure," Mason pointed out. "She could be doing something illegal to make ends meet. Often men labeled as boyfriends are really pimps."

She winced. "I don't want to believe that." Although she couldn't deny that Jose, if that's who she saw in the apartment last night, hadn't acted like a boyfriend. Her chest tightened. Maybe he was something else to Nanette.

Something dangerous.

If only Nanette had come to her, she'd have gladly helped the single mom and the ten-year-old out. But it was too late for regrets. They had little choice but to move forward from here.

"Aubrey?" Mason stared at her.

"You might be right," she was forced to admit. "I don't like it, but I can't argue your logic."

"That's exactly why I follow people, to get to the truth. You'd be surprised at how many people lead double lives."

Mason scanned the street. "We can keep going, but I'm not sure what we'll gain from this. We may need to regroup and form a new plan of attack."

"Okay, where do you want to go?"

"First, we need to hike back to the SUV." He offered a rare smile. "Bravo's nose took us pretty far out of the way."

Swallowing a groan, she nodded. Apparently, her routine walk to and from work hadn't prepared her for the physical exertion of tracking Lucas. No doubt she was holding Mason back. He'd have covered the ground today much faster without her. They'd only been looking for a few hours, and she was already exhausted.

Granted, she'd also been shot at twice in less than twelve hours. Dodging gunmen took a toll physically and emotionally. She was hanging on by a thread. Maybe Mason was paranoid, but she was only alive now because of his strength and skill.

The thought was sobering. It wasn't a matter of if the next attack would come, it was more about when and where it would happen.

And these frequent attacks against her did not bode well for the outcome of their search.

Still, she wasn't about to let her lack of physical fitness get in the way of finding out what had happened to the boy.

While praying with all her heart and soul that he was alive and unharmed.

MASON SWEPT his gaze over the area as he led the way back to his SUV. He wished Kaleb would hurry up and get there. It grated knowing Aubrey was in harm's way. When his phone vibrated, he'd thought for sure Kaleb would be calling, but it was Detective Russo.

He lifted the phone to his right ear. He could hear fine with the volume on high. "Another gunman?" Russo demanded.

"Yes." He drew Aubrey and Bravo into a narrow opening between two buildings. Having one deaf ear, he didn't dare walk and talk on the phone at the same time, fearing someone would manage to approach on his bad side. "Did you find the vehicle?"

"Yes, it was abandoned just outside the park with a bullet hole in the engine. The crime scene techs are checking for prints. But what on earth are you doing in East Village?" Russo demanded.

"Looking for Lucas." He decided there was no point in beating around the bush. He expected Russo to unleash a tirade, but surprisingly, the guy didn't.

"I know you're a SEAL, but this is a job for law enforcement."

"True, but I have Bravo, a trained K9 tracker. Besides, it can't hurt to have more eyes out there searching for this boy."

In his peripheral vision, he saw Aubrey leaning against the wall, nodding in agreement.

Russo sighed loud enough that he could hear him. "I can't have you going all commando on me, Gray." There was a pause, then the detective added, "I suppose you're armed."

"Yes." Again, no reason to deny the truth. "I'm not planning to go commando, as you put it, but this kid is deaf, which makes him more vulnerable than most. There may be a chance Bravo can find him."

"I know. I've got a twelve-year-old, so this situation hits

close to home for me too. Just—keep me updated on any progress you make."

"I will. And while I know I'm just another civilian, I'd appreciate any information you uncover."

"Yeah, I'll do that. My boss won't like it, but I don't care. The kid's welfare comes first. Later." Russo abruptly disconnected from the line.

He glanced at Aubrey. "That was Russo, the vehicle was found and is being checked for fingerprints. Maybe they got sloppy since I'm sure they abandoned the car in a hurry."

"It sounds as if he's okay with us working the case," Aubrey noted.

Us? Mason swallowed the urge to correct her and simply nodded. "Yeah. He has a twelve-year-old and agreed the kid's safety trumps the rules." Mason also figured his being a retired Navy SEAL helped. He doubted Russo would have offered to share information with any other civilian out looking for the boy. "Ready to go?"

"Yes." She pushed herself upright.

He led the way, sweeping his gaze over the area. Now that the guys in the vehicle knew he was armed and willing to shoot, he didn't think they'd be so eager to come after them so soon. Yet he refused to leave anything to chance. Preparation and training were the keys to success. That and always expecting the unexpected.

". . . longer," Aubrey said.

He turned to face her. "Sorry, I didn't catch that."

"We should keep searching a while longer," she repeated. "Bravo has already given us a few clues. Maybe Lucas is being kept in a warehouse or something nearby."

"Not now." He didn't want to admit that once Kaleb showed up, he planned to take Bravo out on his own to continue searching for the boy. Leaving Aubrey home alone wasn't an option, but he trusted Kaleb and Sierra to protect her.

For a moment, Kaleb's tanned skin and bleach-blond hair flashed in his mind. Would Aubrey find him attractive? Kaleb had been one of the guys who'd gotten married when they were young only to end up divorced two years later. The guy was also a chick magnet.

Wait a minute, was he jealous? Talk about losing his mind. Since when did he care enough about a woman to be jealous of the attention she gave to his teammates?

Never.

Until now.

He told himself to shake it off. Getting emotionally involved wasn't smart. He needed to keep calm and focused.

The SUV appeared to be undisturbed, but he still held up a hand, preventing Aubrey from getting too close. "Bravo, sit. Guard."

The dog sat directly in front of Aubrey, his ears perked forward as if anticipating the attack command.

Mason walked around the vehicle, closely examining each nook and cranny. When he didn't find anything, he stretched out on the ground, face up, and shimmied beneath the car. Using his phone flashlight app, he scrutinized the undercarriage.

The vehicle was clear. No tracking device and no bomb. He scooted out and rolled to his feet. Bravo looked as if he hadn't moved a muscle.

He opened the passenger door. "You can get in now."

Aubrey's hazel eyes were wide. "Did you really expect to find something under there?"

"I always expect the worst."

She paused beside him, resting her hand on his arm. Her empathetic gaze locked on his. "I'm sorry you've had to live that way, Mason."

Sorry? He arched a brow, trying to ignore how much he liked the warmth of her touch. "I'm not. I'm alive because I've learned to live this way."

She winced. "Of course, I'm very happy you're here with me. But being that suspicious all the time . . ."

"Is second nature." The last thing he wanted or needed was pity. "Please, get inside. I need to put Bravo in the back."

She nodded and released his arm to slide into the passenger seat. He closed her door and signaled for Bravo to follow him.

He wasn't sure why her comment irked him. After getting Bravo settled, he climbed in behind the wheel and pulled into traffic. Keeping one eye on the rearview mirror for a possible tail, he headed back to his place.

"I'm sorry if I upset you."

Mason swallowed a sigh. He had to admit, he wasn't accustomed to talking about his feelings like this. "You didn't. But don't expect me to apologize for who I am."

"I don't expect that at all," she protested.

"I'm fine," he repeated firmly, hoping she'd drop it. "Are you hungry? We can stop and pick up something for lunch on the way."

"A salad would be nice." Aubrey suddenly straightened in her seat and tapped her passenger-side window. "There he is!"

"Who?" He glanced where she indicated.

"Jose! I'm sure it's him. Turn around, hurry!" She pressed her face up against the window. "I'm sure it's him. He's going into that dark brown building."

Her words were muffled, but he got the gist. Cranking the wheel, he made a quick U-turn. The building's windows were boarded up, but apparently the door worked because he caught a glimpse of a short, stocky Hispanic man disappearing inside.

"I can't figure out what kind of business it is," Aubrey said. "There's no sign on the door."

If it was used for drug dealing or something equally illegal, there wouldn't be a sign, but Mason kept that thought to himself. He found a spot where he could park the SUV while keeping the door in sight.

"Let's go," Aubrey said the moment he shifted the car into park.

"Not so fast." He held on to her arm, preventing her from jumping out of the car. "Let's see if he comes out."

"What if he has Lucas in there?" Aubrey tried to shake off his grip. "We can't just sit here."

"Have patience, if Lucas is in there, we'll get him out." He kept his tone reassuring. "But first we need to know how many other people are inside. I'm not risking Bravo's life if there are six armed men surrounding the kid."

She immediately went still. "No, of course not." She shook her head and slumped against the seat. "I guess I didn't think it through."

"That's my job. Yours is to follow orders." The corner of his mouth quirked up in a reluctant smile since, really, she hadn't followed any of his orders yet. "Let's give Jose a few minutes, see if he comes out."

As he'd suspected, it didn't take long for the door of the boarded-up building to open again. Jose stepped out and glanced both ways as if checking for cops before hunching his shoulders and heading north.

He put the car into drive and pulled out of the parking

space. Jose wasn't walking fast, and having a car keep pace would be too noticeable. Yet he also didn't want to lose him.

Jose continued walking down the street, oblivious to their presence. As he drove, Mason went through a couple of possible scenarios.

If he didn't have Aubrey with him, this would be easier. But he could still pull over and jump out in time to grab the guy. Even if Jose took off running, he didn't doubt he'd be able to overtake him. It wasn't as if Jose was in tip-top shape.

There was a bulge beneath his light jacket that Mason suspected was a gun. No way was he sending Bravo after the guy.

He spied an opening between cars a little ahead of Jose. He sped up and quickly nosed the vehicle into the spot. "Get behind the wheel. If anything happens, call 911."

"Wait, where are you—" He didn't wait for her to finish.

Pausing between the cars, he eyed Jose. The guy appeared to be mumbling to himself and paused beneath a round half-lit sign of a tavern. He quickly stepped out onto the sidewalk before the guy had a chance to duck inside the bar. "Jose?"

The stocky man jerked at the sound of his name, paled, and turned to run. By then, Mason had already grabbed the back of his jacket, forcing him up against the brick wall.

"You're not going anywhere." He quickly disarmed the man, putting the small pistol in his waistband. "Now, tell me where Lucas Espinoza is."

"I don't know . . ."

Mason pressed the man's face more firmly into the building. "Don't waste my time," he hissed. "Where's Lucas?"

"I—think the *Diablos Azules* have him," Jose mumbled.

"The Blue Devils? Who are they?"

"Please, they'll kill me . . ."

He saw movement from the corner of his eye at the same time Aubrey shouted, "Mason, look out!"

He whirled around in time to see a group of six angry-looking Hispanic men coming toward him, each of them with weapons tucked into their waistbands.

If he was alone, he'd stand his ground. But having Aubrey meant it was time to retreat. He shoved Jose to the ground, then pulled his weapon to fire at the sign over their heads. The gunshot and bits of sign raining down on their heads made them scatter. He leaped into the passenger seat. "Go," he roared.

Aubrey hit the gas and pulled into traffic. He mentally braced himself for return fire, hoping a secondary escape plan wouldn't be needed.

CHAPTER FIVE

Gripping the steering wheel, Aubrey did her best to avoid crashing the SUV while getting away from the men with guns. Her heart thundered in her chest, making it impossible to draw in a deep breath.

"It's okay, we're fine now." Mason reached over to lightly touch her arm.

Unwilling to tear her gaze from the road, she gave a nod to indicate she heard him. Desperate to feel safe, she took a left turn, then another right, mimicking his driving maneuvers from the day before.

Finally, she slowed the car, pulled over, and turned in her seat to look at him. He cocked his head so that his right ear was close to her. "Why did you shoot at the sign?"

"To scare them off." Mason appeared ridiculously calm after the hair-raising encounter. She supposed that his interaction with Jose was nothing more than a friendly chat compared to what he'd faced while serving his country. "And it worked."

No denying that. "What was that Jose said about Lucas? The devils have him?"

"The Blue Devils, which I believe may be some sort of local gang," he confirmed.

"A gang?" She stared in horror. "That's terrible."

"It's a lead," he countered. "Not that we can necessarily believe Jose was telling the entire truth, but he was scared. Claimed the Blue Devils would kill him if he talked."

A large knot formed in her stomach. She didn't know much about gangs, but the thought of Lucas being handed over to them made her feel sick. His deafness meant it would be far more difficult for him to figure out what was going on.

She reminded herself that Lucas was smart. He could read lips, maybe not as well as she could, but every deaf person figured out that was the easiest way to understand those who could hear.

"Don't, Aubrey," Mason said. "Going through the worst-case scenarios isn't helpful. If Lucas was taken by gang members, then it's highly likely he's still alive. And that's far better than the alternative, isn't it?"

"Yes." Her tone lacked conviction. If they physically abused him or . . . no. She gave herself a mental shake. Don't go there. Mason was right. Imagining the worst wouldn't help.

They needed to find him.

"If you don't mind, I'll drive from here," Mason said, breaking into her thoughts.

"Okay." When Mason got out of the car, she climbed over the center console. She clasped her fingers together to prevent them from trembling. "Have you heard of the Blue Devils?"

"No, but we'll check in with Russo and Lee about that." Mason grimaced as he pulled into traffic. "I'm irked that I had to let Jose go without getting more information from him."

"Maybe that tavern is his hangout?"

He shrugged. "Maybe once, but I doubt he'll go back there anytime soon. Especially if those guys know he talked to us."

The knot in her stomach tightened painfully. "Do you think they'll hurt Jose?"

"I hope not." Mason glanced at her. "You can't worry about everyone, Aubrey. Jose is likely the reason Lucas is missing in the first place. If he is involved with the Blue Devils, he needs to get himself out."

Logically, she knew he was right. She couldn't save everyone from their poor choices, especially an adult like Jose. Lucas was only a child, he didn't deserve to suffer. Still, she hated knowing that they may have put Jose in danger.

She didn't say anything more as Mason drove them to his house. The nice quiet neighborhood was so different from where they'd been that she felt even more hopeless about Lucas and Nanette's future.

Mason released Bravo from the back, giving the dog time to do his business before heading inside. Moments later, he had his phone to his right ear. "Russo? It's Gray. Call me, we found Jose and learned of a possible lead on Lucas's whereabouts."

They hadn't stopped for food. Aubrey wasn't hungry, but Mason rummaged in his fridge. "I have some leftover chicken noodle soup along with the fixings for ham and cheese sandwiches."

"Whatever you'd like is fine. Would you like help?"

"No thanks."

She dropped into a chair, surprised that Bravo came

over to stretch out beside her. He'd done good work today finding clues about Lucas. Maybe once they located the hangout for the Blue Devils, he'd lead them to the boy.

Then she remembered the six men with bulges beneath their shirts who'd approached Mason and Jose. Six armed men against one. She shivered at the close call.

On second thought, they'd be better off sending the police to the Blue Devils' hideout, not Mason and Bravo. Bad enough that she'd dragged Mason into her mess. Risking his life and that of his dog more than necessary was unacceptable.

By the time Mason had heated up the soup and made the sandwiches, her appetite had returned. He set the meal on the table, and she reached over to take his hand. "Dear Lord, we ask You to bless this food we are about to eat and to continue keeping Lucas safe in Your care, Amen."

"Amen," Mason echoed.

She was pleased he'd participated in her prayer. When he checked his phone several times while they ate, she asked, "Waiting for Detective Russo to call back?"

"Yeah, and I'm waiting to hear from Kaleb. I expected him to be here by now."

She remembered he'd mentioned his teammate. "Maybe something came up."

A hint of a smile crossed his features. "It would have to be a really important issue to keep him from coming. He may have hit heavy traffic that slowed him down, but he'll come through for me."

His tone was full of conviction, and she wondered what it was like to have friends like that. Once she and Carter had plenty of friends, other married couples they'd gone to college with, but after his death, those connections had eventually withered away. At first, their friends had gone overboard to include her, but when they'd started setting her up with other men, she'd made it clear she wasn't interested. Soon, the women began having babies, which added another level of complexity when it came to getting together.

Being the odd woman out had often felt awkward to the point she'd simply stopped going along. On occasion, the women would call her to have lunch, but even those gatherings had become few and far between, no doubt their kids keeping them busy.

Their lives and families were very different from her solitary existence. Her own fault, she knew. She and a few of the teachers got together on occasion, but she couldn't imagine calling on any of them to help her fight off gunmen while searching for a missing boy.

"Aubrey? Are you okay?"

Mason's question pulled her from her thoughts. "I'm fine. This chicken soup is delicious. Did you make it yourself?"

He nodded. "It wasn't that hard. I like to eat, which meant learning to cook."

"I tend to make easy stuff," she admitted. "Nothing fancy. It's not nearly as much fun to cook for one person."

"How long ago did you lose your husband?"

"Ten years." She shrugged. "A long time ago, yet in some ways it still feels like yesterday."

"You must have loved him very much." Was there a hint of longing in his tone?

"I did, yes." She didn't go on to explain about her late-term miscarriage. That loss on top of Carter's death had hit hard. And she often found herself wondering what they would have done if Carter hadn't suffered the aggressive form of leukemia. Would they have kept trying to have children? Or would they have gone the adoption route?

Carter had wanted a large family, but she was an only child. Early on in their marriage, he'd joked about settling for five kids, but she'd insisted they'd have two.

Then the miscarriages had started. Two before the third one had happened at eighteen weeks.

Now there were none.

Mason's phone rang, startling her so badly she dropped her spoon into her soup, making a mess as the contents splashed up from the bowl.

"You seem tense, Aubrey. Try to relax, we're safe now." He reached for the phone and hit the speaker button. "Russo, thanks for calling me back. By the way, I have you on speaker."

"What's this about you finding Jose, then losing him?" the detective demanded.

"We happened to see him walking toward a tavern, so I took him aside to have a little chat. When I asked where Lucas was, he told me they would kill him if he talked—"

"Who would?" Russo interrupted.

"Are you familiar with the Blue Devils?" Mason asked. "Are they a gang of some sort?"

"Never heard of them," Russo said firmly. "Sounds like Jose was playing you."

"I don't think so, he looked scared to death, and while we were chatting, six guys all carrying guns headed our way. I shot at the sign overhead to scare them off, then we got out of there. That was the only reason I let him go."

"Six guys all carrying?" Russo echoed. He let out a low whistle. "Smart move to shoot at the sign to scare them off. And I have to admit, it does sound like a gang."

"Exactly." Mason held her gaze for a moment. "I have a

buddy coming into town to keep an eye on Aubrey. When Kaleb gets here, Bravo and I will see what we can uncover about the Blue Devils."

Wait a minute. She scowled. "I'm going with you."

Mason shook his head but addressed Russo. "Detective, I need you to find out from your gang task force who the Blue Devils are and what they're involved in. I assume drugs at the very least, maybe some sex trafficking too."

Drugs? Sex Trafficking? She shied away from imagining Lucas being involved in either of those illegal activities.

"I will, but you need to stay out of it now," Russo said. "If gangs are involved, we'll take over from here."

Aubrey could tell by the stubborn expression on Mason's face he wasn't going along with that plan. "I promise to keep you informed. But I need to know if you've learned anything new too. This can't be a one-way street." He paused, then added, "If you don't start sharing, I won't bother contacting you again."

"I don't know much," Russo protested. "The crime scene techs came up with a partial print from the vehicle you shot, but we haven't ruled out the owner of the car yet. So far, we don't have any cooperating witnesses either."

The news was depressing. Aubrey was shocked that she and Mason had found all the clues so far, scant as they were, while the police had come up with zip.

Which didn't say much for their chances of finding Lucas, alive and unharmed.

MASON SWALLOWED A WAVE OF FRUSTRATION. He understood Detective Russo had other cases, and where was Detective Lee anyway?

Maybe they'd split up their caseload, but the lack of progress was not encouraging. For a fleeting moment, he wondered if he should consider applying to be a cop, then quickly dismissed the notion. He was too old, not to mention mostly deaf. Besides, he'd had his fill of taking orders from men who hadn't been in the trenches in years. Even if the San Diego police force took him on, he figured he'd be fired for insubordination within his first week.

Nah, better to head out with Bravo on a solo mission. Having his teammates backing him up would be even better.

"Gray? Are you still there?" Russo asked irritably.

"Yeah, we're here." Aubrey held up the photograph she had of Lucas. "Do you need Lucas's picture? I can text you one."

"His mother gave us one. Stay in touch, Gray, and don't get hurt." Russo disconnected from the call, giving Mason the impression that the detective liked to have the last word.

"You're not going off without me," Aubrey said. "Lucas knows me. He'll feel more comfortable with me. Especially if . . ." Her voice trailed off.

He empathized with her position, he really did. But it just wasn't happening. "Aubrey, I need you to be safe. Worrying about you is distracting."

"But we're a team." Her wide hazel gaze implored him to reconsider. "Please, Mason. I would feel so much better if your friend Kaleb helped us search for Lucas rather than wasting his time and talent babysitting me."

He couldn't argue her logic, but he wasn't willing to cave under pressure either. Aubrey needed to be safe, end of discussion.

When they finished eating, Aubrey insisted on doing

the dishes. Needing some space away from her enticing scent, he went into the living room to call Kaleb.

"Where are you?" Mason demanded.

"Sorry, Chief. I'm still an hour away. Got a late start because Nico called to let me know Ava Rampart is missing."

The news was like a punch to the gut. "Jaydon's sister? When? What happened?"

"I don't have the details yet. Nico apparently stopped in to give Ava his condolences, only she wasn't there. He followed up with Jaydon's mother who claims Ava took off with her boyfriend a couple of weeks ago but hasn't been back since. You remember Jaydon's parents are divorced, and his mother had remarried some guy named Robert last year. Could be Ava didn't get along with the new stepdad."

"Well, she's not a kid, she's thirty-one, right? Eight years younger than Jaydon?"

"I know, but still. You know Nico, he has a bug up his backside about it. Wants to go looking for her. Says that's what Jaydon would want us to do."

"Nico's right about that, Jaydon would expect us to find her," Mason was forced to agree. "Does Nico want you and the other guys to help search for her? I'm tied up with a missing kid here in San Diego, but if you need to head over, that's fine. I totally understand. Our loyalty should be for Jaydon's sister."

There was a pause as Kaleb considered this. "How about I head over to talk to Nico first and follow up with you tomorrow? I'm not sure how the kid plans on finding Ava after a few weeks have gone by, but I feel the need to talk him through this."

"Not a problem," Mason assured him, even though he mentally winced. More one-on-one time with Aubrey was not what he needed. "Where are the others? Hudson, Dallas, and Dawson? Are they able to join you guys?"

"Nico was still tracking them down. Hudd is off-grid these days; we're not sure exactly what's going on with him. Dallas headed home to Texas, and Dawson went to Montana."

The news of Hudson being off-grid was concerning. Hudd had sustained a serious concussion during their last mission and had lost vision in one eye as a result.

Maybe Hudson was struggling to come to grips with his new handicap, the same way Mason was.

A wave of guilt washed over him. If only they'd gotten out of there earlier. If only he'd taken an alternate route. If only . . .

"Chief? You still there?"

"I'm here." He forced the acknowledgment through his tight throat. The guys called him Chief because of his actual navy rank of Senior Chief, which he no longer had now that he'd been medically discharged from the service. "Turn around, Kaleb, and meet up with Nico. Make sure he doesn't go off the deep end on this. It's likely Ava went with her boyfriend willingly, and they may have just decided to relocate."

"Without telling her mom and stepfather?" Doubt laced Kaleb's tone. "I guess anything is possible, but it doesn't sound good."

"The only easy day was yesterday," Mason reminded him, quoting the SEAL mantra. "You guys meet up with Nico and get the lay of the land. But check in with me tomorrow, okay?"

"Will do." Kaleb clicked off.

"I guess that means you're stuck with me, huh?" Aubrey's voice had him glancing up in surprise. He hadn't heard her come in. A common problem when he had his phone up against his good ear.

"My choice to get involved and to protect you," he said calmly. "But to answer your real question, yes, unfortunately we're on our own as Kaleb is tied up for a while."

"You mentioned another woman, Ava?" A tiny frown puckered her brow. "How do you and Kaleb know her? Is she missing too?"

"Ava is Jaydon's younger sister. Jay didn't make it home from our last mission." His fault, but he didn't mention that part. "We don't know for sure that she's missing. Sounds like she took off with her boyfriend and hasn't been in touch with her mother and stepfather since. Jaydon claimed they had a dysfunctional family, but we didn't take that comment seriously. I think the divorce happened when he was in high school and contributed to his joining the navy."

Her frown deepened. "Mason, if you want to go help your SEAL teammates, I'll totally understand. Lucas isn't your problem, he's my student. I'm the one who called Child Protective Services, which likely contributed to whatever happened to him."

He rose to his feet, his gaze narrow. "You don't know me very well if you really think I'd walk away and leave you alone with gunmen stalking you."

She crossed her arms over her chest. "I dragged you into this, Mason. You're going well above and beyond the call of duty in helping me find Lucas."

Funny thing was he didn't feel as if helping her was his duty or obligation. For the first time in the few months he'd been demoted to a civilian, he felt alive.

And yeah, part of that was having a renewed purpose, like searching for Lucas.

But deep down, he suspected the newly awakened feelings swirling inside him were a direct result of spending time with Aubrey, a woman he was absolutely attracted to.

Why now, after so many years of avoiding relationships, he had no clue. It was both frustrating and exhilarating.

"I'm not leaving you," he repeated firmly. "But we need to come up with another strategy. I don't want to wait for Russo or Lee to call us back."

"Too bad we can't find them online," she joked.

"If we knew Jose's last name, we could look him up in the court system, see what's in his criminal history." He pulled out his phone again and called Russo. "Detective? I need Jose's last name."

"And I need a million bucks," the detective shot back. "Seriously, Gray, if I had that, I'd already have him in the box asking questions about the boy."

"There has to be a way to find out if Jose has connections with the Blue Devils," Mason pressed. "You guys should be able to pull that information out of your database."

"Lee is working on that right now," Russo admitted. "We're not just sitting here, twiddling our thumbs."

He rubbed the back of his neck. "I never said you were." Although he may have thought it. "I need something to go on. A place where the Blue Devils hang out. Names of some of their members. Anything."

"Hang on." There were muffled sounds in the background for a few minutes before Russo came back on the line. "We found one guy who was arrested recently with a blue devil tattoo. Perp's name is Francisco Hernandez."

"Send me a picture of the tattoo and of Hernandez's mug shot." He thought back to when he had Jose up against the brick wall of the tavern. He'd glimpsed the tattoo on the back of his neck, the one Aubrey had mentioned, but it hadn't been blue. There were two words written, but they were mostly covered by his hoodie. "It may be similar to what Jose has."

"Ms. Clark couldn't identify his tattoo, other than to say he had one," Russo protested.

"I know, and I didn't get a good look at it earlier today either. But I want to see what the blue devil looks like."

"It's not blue like a blue Smurf if that's what you're thinking," Russo drawled. A moment later, his phone vibrated with an incoming text. "I sent both photos to you. Anything else?"

"Yeah. A location as to where Hernandez was picked up."

Russo tapped computer keys. "He was arrested two weeks ago in East Village outside a bar called Twisted. He's currently out on bail, though."

"That works, thanks." He ended the call and pulled up the text message pictures. The blue devil wasn't completely blue, but it did have a blue crown and a pitchfork with blue flames. Weird, but then again, most gangs used codes in their tattoos to help cover up the real meaning. The image of Hernandez was next. He didn't look Hispanic, except for his brown eyes, but the scar along his cheekbone was memorable. Mason wondered if the scar had contributed to the guy being caught.

Most gang members hid their tattoos so that they weren't visible and therefore easily identified. Victims tended to remember scars too, especially bad ones.

He wondered if Jose and Francisco knew each other. If Jose was a member of the Blue Devils, he assumed they did.

And if Jose wasn't a member of the gang? Was it possible handing Lucas over to the group was some sort of gang initiation?

He decided against mentioning that possibility to Aubrey.

"Can I see?" She crossed over and gestured to the phone.

He handed her the device. She peered at the images for several long moments, focusing more of her attention on Hernandez than on the tattoo. "Have you seen him?"

"I don't think so," she said, reluctantly handing the phone back. "I wish I had."

"Well, he's out on parole, so he's no use to us," Mason said gently. "But I did learn he was arrested outside a bar called Twisted. I'd like you to stay here with Bravo while I check it out."

"I'm going with you," she said, the way he knew she would.

"Aubrey, it's a bar, you'll stick out like a wart on a beauty queen."

"Please don't leave me here, alone, Mason. I'll stay in the car with Bravo if that helps. But I want to be close by."

"Aubrey." He blew out a breath. The woman was driving him nuts, and he really, really wished Kaleb was coming to help. "You'll be here during the daylight with Bravo who will scare off any intruder. The bar could mean nothing, Hernandez was arrested outside the place, not inside."

"I was helpful earlier, driving away from Jose, wasn't I? I followed orders like a good soldier. I promise I won't cause you any trouble," she insisted.

Little did she know she was already causing him a boatload of trouble. Or maybe *angst* was a better word. He was used to having his fellow SEALs covering his six, not a sign language teacher.

"There aren't soldiers in the navy," he said dryly. "We're sailors. And the SEALs are frogmen."

"I stand corrected." Her hazel gaze was impossible to ignore.

"Fine." There was no point in wasting time arguing. Seemed the woman had a core of sheer stubbornness that he had little hope of bending to his will.

No matter how hard he tried.

"Thank you." She caught him off guard by going up on her tiptoes to kiss him. He was sure the gesture was meant to be sweet and friendly, but the moment their mouths met, a sizzling desire hit with the force of tsunami.

As their mouths fused, he wrapped his arms around her waist and pulled her close. She melted against him, participating wholeheartedly in the embrace.

He didn't care if he was drowning. In that moment, he didn't want this impromptu kiss to end.

CHAPTER SIX

Aubrey clung to Mason's broad shoulders, reveling in the heat of his kiss. She'd forgotten what it was like to be held in a man's arms, to be cherished, and to be kissed as if there was no tomorrow.

And she liked it, very much.

Mason finally lifted his head, breaking off the kiss. It took a moment for the haze in her mind to clear. "I—that was amazing."

"I guess that means I don't need to apologize for crossing the line," Mason drawled.

Apologize? She frowned. "I'm pretty sure I kissed you."

"And I'm pretty sure I changed your friendly kiss into something far different," he shot back. He let her go and took a step back, running his hand over his short hair. "Listen, I don't want you to think that I expect anything from you. I only want to keep you safe while finding Lucas. That wasn't an invite or an expectation to something more intimate."

She felt herself blush. "I don't think that at all, and I

would never agree to that type of arrangement." Did he honestly think that was the reason she'd kissed him? How mortifying.

Why on earth had she given in to that impulse anyway? For ten years, she'd been immune to handsome men, until now. This was the wrong time and, really, the wrong man. She didn't believe a tough Navy SEAL would be the least bit interested in a schoolteacher.

The only reason she was here with Mason was because of Lucas. And it was wrong of her to spend one iota of time thinking about how much she wanted to kiss Mason again while Lucas was in danger.

"That's settled then." Mason's abrupt tone made her feel even worse. Did she owe him an apology? After all, she was the one who'd initiated the kiss in the first place. "Are you ready? We need to hit the road."

"Of course." She quickly headed over to grab her small purse and her jacket. "I'm ready. The sooner we find Lucas, the better. Are you familiar with where Twisted is located?"

"No, but I'm sure we'll find it." Mason shrugged into his jacket and clasped a leash to Bravo's collar. "Modern technology is great. My phone will get us there."

They headed back outside. Mason paused, giving Bravo time to water a few scrubby bushes before he put the dog in the kenneled area of this SUV. She slid into the passenger seat, trying not to think about how much she admired Mason. He was so different from anyone she'd ever met, especially the way he'd instantly come to her rescue and jumped in to assist in finding Lucas.

As Mason drove back to East Village, she thought about his going inside the bar alone. "I think you should take Bravo in with you. I'll wait in the car and be ready to call 911 if needed."

"Bravo will stay with you." Mason spoke without looking at her. "I don't want to be worried about you when I'm inside the place, checking it out."

She hated being a liability to him. "Please, Mason, take Bravo with you. I keep remembering how those six men with guns came directly toward you and Jose."

He flicked her an amused glance. "I could have taken them all down, Aubrey. However, I didn't really want to go to jail, which is why I shot at the sign over their heads. The worst that could have happened is that the owners of that fine establishment would make me pay to replace the damaged sign. Trust me, I know how to handle myself."

She didn't doubt he was a highly trained SEAL, but she feared he was underestimating how his hearing loss may work against him. Especially in a crowded bar with a lot of background noise.

Yet she also knew he wasn't going to budge on this issue. Maybe she should have stayed at his place. If anything bad happened to Mason, she'd never forgive herself.

It didn't take long for Mason to find Twisted. He drove slowly past it, and she couldn't help but grimace. The building looked even more decrepit than the place where they'd stumbled across Jose.

There was no parking nearby, forcing Mason to park several blocks away. As he moved to get out of the vehicle, she grasped his arm. "Wait."

He turned to look at her, his expression calm as if he had absolutely no concerns about the danger he was facing.

"Please consider taking Bravo with you, what if Lucas is being held somewhere inside?" She held up her phone. "I've dialed 911 and can press the call button the moment I see anything suspicious. But it's just as important to have

Bravo with you, to find Lucas and to provide backup if needed."

"Your lack of faith in my abilities is troubling," he said wryly. "But I know how to compromise. I'll take Bravo out to see if he alerts near the building. If not, he'll come back to guard you. If he does, I'll take him with me."

"Great." She didn't bother to hide her relief. "It's not that I don't trust your training, it's just that I'm concerned about you."

"Thanks, I think." He slid out of the car, shut the door, and then went around back to let Bravo out. He offered the dog the scent bag containing Lucas's sweatshirt.

"Seek!" he commanded.

As Mason and Bravo moved down to the tavern, she kept her phone in her hand and prayed for God to watch over them.

And to keep Lucas safe from harm too.

Unfortunately, it didn't take long for Mason and Bravo to return. Instead of putting the dog in the back, Mason opened her passenger-side door. "Scoot over, the key fob is in the center console. I want Bravo to be up front with you."

"He didn't pick up Lucas's scent?"

Mason shook his head. She maneuvered over the center console and dropped into the driver's seat. Bravo jumped in and sniffed at her. "Guard, Bravo. Guard."

The dog settled onto his haunches, his head up, his ears perked forward. She wanted to smile at how Bravo seemed to understand everything Mason said, but she couldn't.

"Be careful."

"Always." Mason shut the door and moved back toward the tavern.

This time, the waiting seemed interminable. She kept

up a one-sided conversation with Bravo, who cocked his head at times as if listening to what she was saying.

Which was nothing more than nonsense about how he was to be a good boy and to keep protecting Mason even after they found Lucas and the danger was over. She had to open her window an inch as Bravo's breathing caused them to steam up.

"I'm sure Mason will be back soon," she told Bravo. "He's a smart and strong Navy SEAL. Even with his hearing loss, he'll be able to hold his own. Right?"

Bravo looked from her toward the window and back again. The way he sat there so quiet and intense was a bit unnerving.

"Right." She sighed and glanced around to make sure no one was paying any attention to them. The sun was still high in the sky, although several dark clouds were coming in from the ocean. She loved living in San Diego, mostly because the weather was amazing. Sure, it got cold at night in the winter, but during the day, the temperatures warmed up nicely.

She shrugged out of her jacket and tossed it into the back seat. Bravo leaned over and sniffed her shirt, making her laugh. Then her smile faded as she checked her watch for what seemed like the tenth time in as many minutes.

Mason had only been gone fifteen minutes. She told herself not to worry. That getting information on the Blue Devils would take time. It wasn't as if gang members would discuss their illegal activities with anyone who happened to show an interest.

Just the opposite.

Not that she was an expert on street gangs.

All the more reason the police should be here, digging

for information. She closed her eyes and took a deep breath. Bravo's cold nose touched her cheek.

She turned to the dog and carefully reached over to scratch his ears, mindful of Mason's warning about how the animal was trained to attack on command. Bravo seemed to like being petted, so she continued stroking his soft fur.

"He's going to be okay, right, boy? Yes, he is." She was trying to reassure herself more than the dog.

She still held the phone in her lap, but looking around, she didn't believe anyone would approach the vehicle with Bravo sitting beside her. In fact, a few people gave them a wide berth as they went past, as if unwilling to get too close.

Without warning, Bravo spun to face the passenger window, growling low in his throat. She had the passenger window open about an inch, and his nose was pressed in the opening. She fumbled for her phone while peering past the animal's head to see what had caught his attention.

His growling morphed into staccato barks. Her fingers tightened around the phone as she tried to understand what was going on. Should she call 911? And report what? A growling K9 warning of danger?

Then she saw Jose running away from the SUV as if the Blue Devils were hot on his heels. Bravo barked two more times, then sat and stared through the glass as if waiting for the bad guy to return.

Aubrey swallowed hard and lowered the phone to her lap. No sense in calling 911 about seeing Jose running off. He'd be long gone before an officer could respond.

"Good boy," she praised, stroking his fur. Bravo clearly took his protector role seriously. And she was impressed that he'd recognized Jose's scent from earlier that day.

Then it hit her that Jose may have been in the tavern

and had seen Mason. Or maybe the guy had recognized the SUV.

A flicker of unease washed over her. Seeing Jose twice in a matter of hours seemed like too much of a coincidence. Yet she knew Bravo hadn't alerted to Lucas's scent near Twisted, so what was Jose doing here?

She felt certain Nanette's boyfriend knew more than he'd admitted to. Especially since the six guys had shown up just as Mason had Jose pinned up against the wall. It made her wonder if Jose had sent up some sort of distress signal. Or maybe he was being followed by the Blue Devils too.

Was this only about Lucas being taken by a street gang? Or was there something more going on here? She was starting to think they'd stumbled across something far more complicated than one missing child. As if a missing deaf boy wasn't terrible enough.

The thought made her shiver despite the warmth of the sun beating into the SUV.

Come on, Mason, she silently urged. *Please come back safely!*

MASON TOOK the time to check out the Twisted tavern from the outside, taking note of the rear exit, the one cracked window, and the other two boarded-up ones on the second story. From there, he examined the buildings on either side of the bar. Then went one step farther, checking out the rest of the street. One of the buildings around the corner had a fire escape that led all the way up to the roof. Farther down, there was another building with a fire escape too. Satisfied, he turned back to his main target, the bar called Twisted.

You didn't go into the lion's den without having an escape plan.

He'd shared Aubrey's disappointment that Bravo hadn't alerted on Lucas's scent around Twisted, yet he hadn't really expected to find the boy that easily. No matter what Aubrey had said, he didn't think the Blue Devils were holding the kid above a well-known hangout.

Granted, criminals often made stupid mistakes.

Mason squared his shoulders and approached the main door with the bold confidence of someone who belonged. SEALs were taught to blend into their environment, be it land or sea. He'd decided to treat this like any other op, despite the lack of intel.

And the lack of backup from his team.

The interior of the bar was crowded, even at two in the afternoon on a Thursday. No working class people here, he noted with one swift glance. It seemed like the kind of place where those who had money to spend and no regular work hours chose to hang out. For all he knew, the upper level was where drug business took place.

Mason edged through the crowd until he found a spot at the bar. He didn't drink very often but ordered a beer anyway.

For a moment, the bald bartender with bulging muscles eyed him suspiciously before he reached into the fridge, removed a cold brew, twisted off the cap, and slid the bottle across to him. Mason set cash on the bar, including a tip, gave him a nod, then lifted the bottle to his lips.

Interesting that he'd already been made as an outsider. It wasn't because he was dressed any differently, but more likely because the bartender knew each of the patrons by name or by face. As he raked a gaze over the group, he noted several of the men avoided his gaze. That alone made Mason believe they'd already pigeonholed him as military and/or a cop.

His SEAL tattoo, a three-pronged trident speared through an anchor with an eagle in the background, was on his right bicep and hidden beneath his light jacket. Their entire team had gotten the ink when they were young and eager to proclaim their status as belonging to the military elite. Now he rather wished he'd been smart enough to have resisted temptation.

Moving through the crowd, he found a spot where he could stand with his back against the wall, pretending to drink his beer. There were only two women in the crowd that he could see, both dressed in slinky outfits and high-heeled shoes, showing so much skin that he assumed they were working girls. Good thing he'd convinced Aubrey to stay in the SUV. He'd drawn enough attention as it was; her wholesome looks would have been like carrying a flashing neon light into the place.

The wall behind him vibrated. Instantly, he realized someone had left through the back door, slamming it shut behind them. No one inside the crowded bar paid any attention, but he eased along the way to the rear doorway he'd eyeballed earlier.

Someone had decided to get out of Dodge fearing he was indeed a cop. He wished he knew who'd taken off but soon decided that wasn't important.

Two big burly guys stepped in front of him. "You need to leave," the taller of the two said. "Now."

"Yeah?" Mason couldn't read lips the way Aubrey could, so he cocked his head to hear them better. He shrugged and held up his bottle. "Maybe when I finish my beer."

"Now," the shorter one growled. "Your kind isn't welcome here."

"My kind?" He arched a brow and kept his expression nonchalant. "A guy can't grab a beer after putting in a long day of work?" He held his beer bottle loosely in his right hand, prepared to drop it to fight if needed.

"You're a cop," the taller guy said flatly. "Now move along, little doggie."

"I'm not a cop," Mason replied evenly. "Why don't the two of you move along before someone gets hurt?"

The younger guy smirked. "Big talk from one guy in a group of fifty."

He didn't bother to respond, keeping his gaze squarely on the two men. He fully expected one or both of them to throw a punch, and they didn't disappoint. Guys like these two tended to use brute force rather than finesse.

The taller man swung at Mason's head while the shorter guy aimed for his gut. Mason had dropped his beer bottle before either of them noticed, and in two swift moves, he'd blocked both blows. Then he sent the shorter guy sailing backward with a kick while grabbing the taller guy and swinging him around so that Mason had his head locked with his arm around this throat, cutting off his air, and his weapon in his left hand pointing at the crowd.

"Back off," he barked as several guys turned toward the commotion. Then he took several steps backward, dragging the taller guy with him toward the rear door.

The short guy was clutching his gut, his face turning green with the need to puke. Mason knew the short guy wasn't going to be a problem, yet he kept his Sig Sauer trained on the crowd as he left the building, dragging the tall dude along with him.

Outside, he spun the guy away from him and threw him up against the wall, much the way he had Jose earlier that day. When the tall guy's face smashed into the brick, blood spurted from his nose. Mason wrenched tall guy's arm up behind his back, keeping him pinned in place. He found the small gun and removed it from the guy's waistband, tucking it into his own.

At this rate, he'd have a whole cadre of illegal weapons.

"You want to tell me why you think I'm a cop?" Mason demanded.

"You broke my nose," tall guy whined.

Mason shook his head at the stupidity of some people. Starting a fight when you're a wimp wasn't smart, which happened a lot with guys who thought a fight was all about muscle without understanding the value of self-defense and a counterattack. These guys wouldn't last one day in BUD/S training. He pressed the guy's face into the brick while keeping an eye on the exit. He figured it wouldn't be long before several others came out to see what had happened to tall guy. "Why?"

"I—heard you were looking for a missing kid," the man confessed.

Mason had wondered about that. "I see you talked to Jose."

The guy didn't respond, but from the involuntary movement of his arm, Mason knew he'd pegged it right.

"Are you with the Blue Devils?" He was running out of time, the guy's buddies would show up at any moment. He wrenched his arm up harder. "Are you?"

"I—I . . ." The rear door of the tavern opened, and three men strolled out.

In a swift move, Mason jerked tall guy from the wall and held him in front of him, his weapon trained on the trio. "Move along, this doesn't concern you."

"Let him go." The largest of the three pulled a gun.

Mason didn't hesitate to fire, hitting him in the arm holding the weapon. The gun fell to the pavement as the guy howled in pain. Mason looked at the other two. "I'm a former Navy SEAL. I can kill you in less than three seconds or you can leave. Your choice."

The largest guy held on to his bleeding arm, his face mottled with rage. "You're going to pay for that!"

"Let's go, Hank." The larger man's two friends dragged him away, clearly not willing to call his bluff.

"Are they Blue Devils too?" Mason asked. He could see the tattoo on the back of tall guy's neck. It was exactly the same as the image Russo had sent him, complete with the blue crown on the devil's head. "You've got the tat, so there's no reason to lie."

"Yes," the tall guy finally admitted. "We heard Jose told you about us."

Mason didn't like hearing that. "Did you do something to Jose because of me? Did you hurt him?"

The guy didn't say anything. Mason put the gun up to his temple. "What did you do to him?"

"Nothing! He took off before they could make him pay!"

How long ago? Mason wondered. Had Jose been the one who left the bar shortly after he'd gone inside? "Are you saying the Blue Devils will kill him over this?"

"I—don't know," the guy whined. "Maybe. Nobody is supposed to talk to the cops."

"Will they do the same to you?" Mason asked in a

dangerously soft voice. "After all, everyone inside Twisted saw you come outside with me."

"I haven't told you anything," the guy protested.

"Jose didn't tell me anything either. But that doesn't really matter, I'll make sure they believe you sang like a jail-bird." Mason didn't have any intention of doing that, but he needed this guy to believe him. He pressed the gun more firmly against his left temple. "You may as well tell me where Lucas is. I can shoot you and leave you here. I doubt anyone from the bar is going to call the police."

"I don't know!" The guy sounded panicked. "I only heard about the kid!"

"What exactly did you hear?" Mason asked. Honestly, he was getting tired of this dude dragging his feet. He brought up his knee, hitting him in the kidney.

"Owwww," he wailed. "Okay, okay, all I know is *El Jefe* wanted him. He told Jose to bring the kid to him."

Mason didn't like the sound of that. Why would the head of the Blue Devils want Lucas? It didn't make any sense. "What's *el jefe's* name?"

"I don't know!" The guy was so tense now that Mason tended to believe him. "I swear I don't know. No one asks questions about *El Jefe*, not unless you want your throat cut and your body tossed in the ocean as shark food."

"Why does the head of the Blue Devils want a deaf boy?" Mason pressed. "You have to give me something to go on, or there's no reason for me to let you live."

"I don't know." The guy was starting to sound like a broken record. "We take orders, we don't ask questions. But if you ask me, it seems *El Jefe* is trying to get into the sex-trafficking business. And a deaf boy can't talk, right?"

Not reassuring news, but then again, not too surprising either. It was one of the scenarios he and Aubrey had feared from the very beginning. "Where can I find *el jefe*? Where's his hangout?"

"I'm not high enough in the organization to have that info." Sweat was pouring off the guy now, and his body was beginning to shake. Mason had to assume tall guy was more afraid of *el jefe* than him. "Go ahead and shoot me, I've told you everything I know." The guy went lax as if giving up the fight.

Mason highly doubted the guy was being completely honest, but he'd learned enough for now, and he didn't want to hang around longer than necessary. Yet before he could release the guy, the rear door of the tavern opened, and three more big dudes emerged. Mason figured the previous guys had gotten a message to them about his questioning tall guy and shooting one of them in the arm.

Without waiting for them to say anything, Mason abruptly shoved tall guy at them with enough force to knock them back a few steps. Then Mason whirled and took off running, following his preplanned escape route.

Gunfire erupted behind him, sounding like muffled fireworks with his hearing loss. Mason ignored the sounds, knowing better than to slow down or look back behind him. Moving was the key, especially since he doubted these guys were accustomed to aiming at a running target. Bullets pinged off the brick, sending shards flying in the air, a few striking his face. He took one corner, then went down to the next building. When he reached the rickety fire escape, he leaped up and grabbed the lower bar and quickly hauled himself up.

Good thing his physical strength hadn't been hampered as much on that last mission the way his hearing had been.

More gunfire popped from the ground, but he easily maneuvered the fire escape, going higher and higher until he was nearly at the roof of the building. Even then, he didn't stop but dashed across the rooftop to the next building over.

The gap was wider than he'd anticipated, but that was okay. Adrenaline surged through his bloodstream. Mason ran straight to the edge of the building and launched himself over the gap, landing with a jarring thud. He tucked, rolled, then kept running to the next building. By his earlier reconnaissance, he knew the third building over would bring him close to where Aubrey waited in his SUV.

He had to reach her before the gunmen did.

CHAPTER SEVEN

Aubrey's heart had lodged in her throat when Bravo began to bark. She'd turned in her seat to see what had caught his attention when she'd heard the gunfire. Instantly, she fumbled for the phone to call 911.

"Shots fired near a tavern called Twisted," she said breathlessly. She knew the gunfire was meant for Mason.

"Are you safe?" the calm female voice asked.

It wasn't easy to hear the dispatcher over Bravo's barking. The dog clearly sensed Mason was in danger. "Yes, but others are in danger. Please hurry!" She didn't bother to stay on the line but dropped the phone and started the SUV.

"Easy, Bravo. Let's stay calm."

The dog continued barking, and it occurred to her that as a SEAL K9, he may be reacting to the sound of gunfire.

Where should she go? What should she do? Sitting here doing nothing wasn't going to cut it. Granted, Mason had told her to stay in the car and to call 911. Which she'd done. Yet she also wanted to drive around to the front of the tavern, except she couldn't be certain Mason wasn't somewhere else. What if he was running in the opposite direction? Gripping the steering wheel tightly, she tried to think logically.

But it was impossible to keep a clear mind while knowing Mason was in danger.

Please, Lord, keep Mason safe in Your care!

She was just about to pull away from the curb when she saw a man sprinting toward her. Recognizing Mason, she nearly wept with relief. She quickly made sure the doors were unlocked as he barreled toward her.

"Go!" he shouted as he opened the back door and jumped in.

Just like earlier that day, she hit the accelerator and pulled out into traffic as he slammed the door behind him. Thankfully, there weren't many cars on the road. She imagined anyone lurking nearby had taken off upon hearing the gunfire.

Bravo jumped between the seats to pounce on Mason. He rubbed the animal's fur, murmuring something she couldn't hear.

"Are you hurt?" She met his gaze in the rearview mirror. "I heard the shots. I assume they were intended for you."

"I'm fine." A wry grin tugged at the corner of his mouth. "I made sure to have an escape plan."

"You might have clued me in." She scowled, unreasonably angry with him. "I had no idea if I should continue waiting or try to find you. You could have died back there!"

"I didn't." His calm voice only irked her more. "I wish you would trust me, Aubrey. I know how to handle myself, and most of those guys are strictly amateurs."

"Most of them?" Her voice rose so high it squeaked. "It only takes one professional to kill you!"

"I'm fine," he repeated. "And I learned a few things."

She blew out a heavy sigh. Her anger wasn't with him

but rather the entire situation. A deaf ten-year-old boy was missing, and no one seemed to care. The police hadn't come up with much, and she wasn't sure how much more of this investigating on their own she could take.

Teaching school hadn't prepared her for this.

Nothing had prepared her for this.

"Don't you want to hear what I found out?" Mason asked.

"Yes." She pulled herself together. "Oh, Jose ran past. I'm not sure if he saw you and took off or what was going on."

"I think he saw me enter Twisted," Mason confirmed. "I didn't see him leave, but I knew someone had disappeared out the rear door. That's okay, though, because I was able to have a little chat with one of the patrons who had a Blue Devils tattoo."

She met his gaze in the rearview mirror. Bravo was sprawled across Mason's lap as if to keep him there. "Did he tell you where to find Lucas?"

"Not exactly, but he mentioned that *el jefe* instructed Jose to bring Lucas to him." Mason's expression turned grim. "I don't find it at all reassuring that the head of the Blue Devils asked specifically for the boy."

She swallowed hard, her imagination already running wild. Why would the boss want Lucas? Solely because he was deaf? Was there some sort of job that needed to be done that only a deaf kid could do?

If so, she was hard-pressed to come up with one.

Maybe this was an attempt to force Lucas into sex trafficking. That possibility bothered her more than anything.

Please, Lord. Please keep Lucas safe in Your care!

"Aubrey?" Mason's voice broke into her thoughts. "You're going the wrong way."

"Where am I supposed to be going?" Even though she hadn't left the SUV or been inside Twisted gathering information from the Blue Devils, she felt exhausted, as if she'd used up every ounce of her strength. Looking back, she knew Mason had made the right call in forcing her to stay behind.

Maybe she should volunteer to stay back at the house. Then again, she had been able to drive them safely away from the gunfire.

"My place. I think it's time we get Russo and Lee to come over for a face-to-face update." Mason gestured with his hand. "Turn right at the next light. Go up three blocks, then turn left."

She followed his directions, and soon the neighborhood looked familiar. Coming upon Mason's mid-sized white house was a welcome relief. Lucas needed their help, and she wanted nothing more than to find him. Yet she wasn't sure how much more of this cloak-and-dagger stuff she could take.

The police needed to do something. Anything. Finding a missing child, especially one who may have been kidnapped and forced into sex trafficking, was their job. It was beyond frustrating that they weren't doing more to help find him.

When they reached Mason's home, she slid out from behind the wheel and slammed the door with more force than was necessary. She turned to face Mason, surprised to find he was eyeing her warily.

"Are you okay?"

"No. How can I be? We've been searching for Lucas all day and still have no idea where he is or the real name of whoever took him." She knew she sounded cranky, but she couldn't help it.

"I know this isn't easy." His tone was soothing. "Let's go inside. I've called Russo; he and Lee will be here shortly."

"Yeah, fat lot of good that will do," she muttered, following Mason and Bravo inside. She watched as Bravo went from room to room as if making sure no bad guys were hiding nearby.

Dropping into a kitchen chair, she did her best to let go of her anger. Being mad wouldn't help. She needed some of Mason's incredible self-control. He pulled a pitcher of lemonade and poured two glasses. He handed one to her and took a seat to her left. "Someone will know who *el jefe* is. And once we know that, we'll have a good chance of finding Lucas."

"You really think so?" She sipped the tart soft drink.

"I do. SEALs are trained to practice the power of positive thinking. You can't go into a dangerous situation fearing the worst." A hint of a smile tugged at the corner of his mouth. "The Blue Devils aren't as tough as they think they are. I'm sure we'll find him."

They would? Or the police? She feared Mason and Bravo were the only ones with the skill to accomplish this task.

Which didn't say much for the local authorities.

Bravo climbed out from beneath the table and went to stare at the front door. Mason noticed and crossed over to peer through the window. Seconds later, he greeted the detectives and invited them in.

"What's this about gunfire outside of Twisted?" Lee demanded with a scowl.

Mason shrugged. "I poked the hornet's nest, and they tried to sting me. Didn't work, though."

"Hrmph," Lee grunted.

"Why not start at the beginning?" Russo sat across from her. Lee joined him.

Mason dropped beside her. He was close enough to touch, and she found his strength and confidence reassuring. As he described how he'd gone into the tavern and had been approached by two men who'd pegged him as a cop, she couldn't stop herself from reaching over to touch his arm.

He'd given her the whitewashed version of events. The idea of two armed men attempting to force him outside filled her with horror.

"I disarmed them, sent one to the floor, and took the other guy out the back," Mason said. "He had the Blue Devils tattoo on the back of his neck. He explained how Jose is in trouble because he was seen talking to me. Then he told me Lucas was taken by *el jefe*. We need to know who runs the Blue Devils."

"Who shot at you?" Lee asked in confusion.

"Three guys who came out of the tavern to help their buddy." Mason shrugged. "I shot one of them in the arm, and they took off. Then three more dudes came out, so I threw my hostage at them and ran. That's when they started shooting."

"You shot someone?" Aubrey tightened her grip on Mason's arm. "You didn't tell me about that."

"Had to, he was pointing his gun at me." Mason waved a hand. "That's not important, it was only a flesh wound, and I highly doubt he plans to press charges. In fact, he'll avoid going in for treatment as all gunshot wounds have to be reported to the police." He eyed the two detectives. "You should put the word out at all the local hospitals, though, just in case. Maybe we'll get lucky and he'll go in. It would be nice to have a name."

Russo nodded. "I will, but you need to stand down on this investigation of yours, Gray. That was a close call back there. You were outnumbered and outgunned. Things could have turned out very differently."

Aubrey found herself nodding in agreement. "Bravo started barking, even before the gunfire. I had the window open, so I don't know if he caught your scent, Mason, or what, but he went crazy. Then the gunfire started, and that only made him bark more. I was scared to death something bad had happened to you."

"Have you found Lucas?" Mason asked, staring intently at both detectives. He covered her hand with his as if to reassure her.

The two men glanced at each other. "No," Russo admitted. "But we are tracking down any and all connections to the Blue Devils."

"Do you know where their leader is? His legal name? Anything?" Mason pressed.

"Not yet." Russo spread his hands. "As you discovered firsthand, it's not easy turning these gang members against each other. So far, we haven't been able to get anyone to talk. But that doesn't mean we're giving up."

"We care about this kid as much as you do," Lee added.

Aubrey doubted that but didn't bother to argue. "What about his mother, Nanette? Have you talked to her again? Maybe she knows why the Blue Devils took her son."

"We went by her apartment twice, but she hasn't answered the door." Russo turned to look at her. "Maybe you should try. She may open up to you."

"Not sure about that." Mason glanced at her.

"Yes, I'm willing to try." She pulled out her phone and called Nanette. As before, the call went straight to voice mail. "Nanette, this is Aubrey Clark from the Stanley

School for the Deaf. Will you please call me? I'm very worried about Lucas, and I want to help you. Thanks." She lowered the device. "I have a feeling she's hiding out somewhere. We went by the restaurant where Nanette works earlier today, the hostess said Nanette wasn't working and that she had off the next few days."

The detectives exchanged a look. Lee asked, "Why didn't you tell us where she worked?"

"I didn't know the name of the restaurant," she said defensively. "Bravo followed Lucas's scent there, and I recognized the uniform."

Both men looked at the dog. Bravo sat straight and tall, ears perked forward. He looked alert as if just waiting for one of them to make a wrong move.

"As I mentioned before, Bravo's expertise is scent tracking. The sooner you locate the main hideout for this gang or the name of the leader of the Blue Devils, the sooner I can use Bravo to find Lucas."

"Before something terrible happens to him," she added. "There has to be a reason the boss asked for him. We're afraid . . ." She couldn't finish the sentence. A ball of emotion hit hard. Tears pricked her eyes. She jumped up from the table and ran into the bathroom as tears rolled down her cheeks.

MASON STOOD, watching as Aubrey disappeared into the bathroom. He understood her fears, even shared them, but his training was such that he couldn't allow emotion to interfere with his mission.

He turned his gaze to the detectives. "Please tell me you found something of interest in the past few hours."

Lee looked affronted, but Russo nodded. "The partial print in the abandoned vehicle belongs to Raymond Nassar. We have a BOLO out for him. Every officer has his mug shot. If he's out and about, we'll find him."

"I'd like a copy of that mug shot," he said.

"I'm not sure about that . . . ," Lee protested, but Russo picked up his phone. A few seconds later, Nassar's face popped up on the screen.

"Do you recognize him?" Russo asked, his gaze intense. "Was he one of the patrons inside Twisted?"

Mason sighed and shook his head. Of course, it wouldn't be that easy. "I don't recognize him, sorry. But you can be sure I'll keep looking for him."

"We've got that covered," Lee said. When Russo shot him an annoyed glance, he quickly added, "Thanks. We'll take all the help we can get."

Yeah, Mason was sure they would. He was glad to have one name and a face, but it wasn't much. He considered heading back to Twisted to ask about Nassar but then decided the risk outweighed the benefit.

Aubrey emerged from the bathroom, her eyes red and puffy from crying. He hated seeing her so upset and went over to meet her. "Aren't you the one who believes that God is watching over us? You have to trust in Him, Aubrey."

"I know." Her attempt to smile was rather pathetic. "I'm trying, but I just keeping thinking that the only reason the Blue Devils would want a deaf kid is to make him do something bad."

"Going down that path will only make it harder to stay focused." He lightly grasped her shoulders and looked into her wide hazel eyes. "We will find him. We have a name and a mug shot of one of the Blue Devils who were in the car that shot at us."

"Not Jose?" Aubrey asked.

"A guy named Raymond Nassar." He showed her the mug shot. "Does he look familiar?"

She examined the photo for a long moment, then shook her head. "No, sorry."

He hadn't expected her to recognize him and slid the phone back into his pocket. The urge to kiss her again was strong. How and why this woman had gotten under his skin, he wasn't sure. He didn't much like it.

"Mason?" She tapped his arm. "The detectives are talking to you."

He turned back to face the kitchen, drawing Aubrey with him. He'd been so engrossed in her that he'd almost forgotten about them. "I'm sorry, I didn't catch that."

"We need to get back to work," Russo said. "But I want you to stay in touch. Especially if you obtain key information."

"Why haven't you gotten key information on where Lucas is being held?" Aubrey's tone was exasperated. "Mason has learned more today than you have, when it should be the other way around."

Lee flushed, but Russo simply nodded. "I agree with you. We've had officers canvassing Lucas and Nanette's neighborhood, but so far without success. We're also questioning all Blue Devils in custody, but none of them are talking either."

"All the officers have Raymond Nassar's mug shot," Mason added. He shared her frustration, but hammering these two wouldn't help. "Hopefully, they'll pick him up very soon."

"That won't help if he doesn't tell us what we need to know," she protested. "You would think those who are already in jail would be more likely to say something."

The gang mentality wasn't all that different from the terrorists he and his team had shut down. Most of them would die to protect their leader. Mason knew what they needed here was someone who had nothing to lose. Who had already been targeted by the Blue Devils.

Someone like Jose.

"We need to find Jose. Word on the street is that *el jefe* has targeted him because he was seen talking to me." He looked at the detectives. "You must have some way of finding his last name and last known address."

"There are hundreds of men named Jose in the system," Lee said dryly.

"I asked our tech guys to run a list of those named Jose with a tattoo. From there, we may be able to narrow it down to those with a known Blue Devils tat," Russo added. "But that's iffy as most tattoos aren't described in detail."

"Of course not," Aubrey muttered. "That would be too easy."

"Please keep us updated on your progress," Mason said as he led them to the door. "And I'll do the same."

Bravo stood beside him as he closed and locked the front door. As much as he wanted to continue searching for Lucas, he didn't think Aubrey was up to the task. He wished Kaleb or any of the other guys were there, but he wasn't going to call them away from searching for Jaydon's sister, Ava, either.

"Now what?" Aubrey asked, her expression strained. "Do we head out to look for this Raymond Nassar guy?"

"Not now." He gently led her back to the kitchen. "We'll stay here for a while. Maybe the cops will pick him up."

"Don't hold your breath." Instead of taking a seat, she crossed her arms over her chest, staring him down. "Besides, we can't stop now, Mason. I have no faith in Russo and Lee. I'd have thought they'd have more information by now. One name of one guy who probably knows nothing about Lucas isn't much."

"Don't forget, Nassar was likely the one who took a shot at us at your place and again in East Village. He's involved in this."

"Probably on *el jefe's* orders," she said grimly. Then her expression turned troubled. "You really think Jose is in danger?"

"Yeah." He couldn't lie to her. "If there was a way to track him down, we might be able to get more information out of him. Especially if there was a way to offer him protection from retribution."

"Protection." She snorted. "That's great, considering he's the one who turned Lucas over to the Blue Devils in the first place." She shook her head and sank into a chair. "I'm worried sick about Lucas."

"I know." It was too early to eat dinner, and like her, he couldn't stand the idea of not keeping up the search. "I'd like you to stay here with Bravo while I head back to East Village."

"What are you planning?"

"I'd like to go back to Nanette's apartment building." He knew how to pick locks and figured it was well past time to get inside the place. Since he wasn't a cop, he wasn't bound by the rules of evidence. Not that he wanted to create problems if the police did eventually get Nanette in custody, but he was fresh out of alternatives.

And he wasn't above breaking and entering to find Lucas.

"I'll go with you," Aubrey said, although she looked exhausted by the mere thought.

"You should stay here with Bravo, he'll protect you. If you use this hand signal"—he showed it to her—"he'll attack the threat. You'll be safe here."

"Are you sure about that?"

He wished he could be 100 percent sure, but he wasn't. There was a slim possibility one of the gang members had gotten his SUV plate number. But he didn't honestly believe they had the connections to trace his license plate to his name and address. As a former SEAL, he wasn't listed anywhere.

"I know you think I'm needy, but I don't want to be left behind, Mason." Her troubled gaze ripped at his heart. "Please. I'd rather wait in the car than sit here."

He wrestled with himself for several tense moments, then reluctantly nodded. It seemed he couldn't deny Aubrey anything.

A *dangerous habit*, he silently admitted. Deep down, he knew he cared more about Aubrey's safety than anything.

Even Lucas.

He grabbed his lock-picking tools and headed outside. It didn't take long to drive back to East Village, and he purposefully parked a few blocks over from the Espinoza apartment building.

"Stay here, Bravo will protect you." He slid out from behind the wheel. It was four o'clock in the afternoon now, and the sun was mostly hidden by clouds, making the sky darker than usual.

After pulling on his gloves, he carefully approached the building, taking note that there were no lights shining through the windows. It was possible she was hiding in the darkness, but he didn't think so. He feared the Blue Devils had come for her, too, although he hadn't mentioned that to Aubrey.

She was stressed enough about Lucas, no need to add that to her plate.

The lock on Nanette's door was easy to bypass. He eased inside, then softly closed the door behind him. He waited a few moments for his eyes to adjust, then moved through the small kitchen to the main living room.

A quick yet thorough search proved the place was empty. Using a small pen flashlight, he searched for something that might give them a hint as to where Lucas, and Nanette for that matter, might be.

No surprise to find a beer coaster from Twisted. Jose likely had hung out there until he'd become persona non grata with the Blue Devils. He found another coaster from a place called The Overlook. He snapped a picture of it, then moved on. He didn't find anything of note in Lucas's bedroom, so he moved on to Nanette's room.

There he found a photo of Lucas, the same one Aubrey had. It was probably a school photo. He picked it up, then frowned. Was there another picture behind it? He undid the back of the frame, and a smaller photo fell out. This one was of Nanette holding a baby in her arms, standing beside a tall Hispanic man. Lucas's father? It seemed likely.

He snapped a picture of the photograph before putting the frame back together.

He wanted to kick himself in the rear end for not thinking of Lucas's father sooner. It was a good clue, and one he thought may help them find the boy.

After slipping from the apartment and relocking the door behind him, he headed back the way he'd come. But when he heard Bravo's frenzied barking, he broke into a run.

CHAPTER EIGHT

Aubrey had chosen to climb over the console to drop into the driver's seat again, with Bravo sitting beside her. When the dog started to bark furiously, she peered beyond him to see what had caught his attention.

Three men were walking down the street toward them. From this distance, though, she couldn't tell if one of them was Jose.

Her heart pounding, she scrunched down in her seat. Should she call 911? And report what? Three men were bothering the dog? Still, it didn't seem prudent to stay there either. She pushed the button to start the engine and eased the gearshift to drive.

As the men drew closer, she realized they all had guns. What was it about this area of the city? She'd lived most of her adult life in San Diego, and she'd never seen anyone carrying a weapon. Then again, maybe people had been carrying without her knowing.

One of the men reached for the gun at his waist. That was all she needed. She hit the gas and cranked the wheel to pull into the road. There wasn't a lot of traffic, which was good.

But she was leaving Mason behind, which wasn't good. She turned right at the next intersection, heading toward Nanette's apartment building, hoping and praying she'd see Mason.

Bravo hadn't stopped his crazy barking, clawing at the window as if desperate to get out of the SUV. Aubrey wasn't sure if she should let him go. Bravo would likely find Mason easily enough, but what if one of the three men shot the dog?

No, she couldn't risk it. Mason wouldn't want her to put Bravo in danger.

A dark figure running caught her attention. Mason! She hit the brake, pulled over to the curb, and unlocked the doors. As before, he yanked open the rear passenger door and jumped in. "Go!"

She hit the gas, careening away from the curb, nearly sideswiping another vehicle. Still, she kept going, anxious to put distance between them and the three men who'd caused Bravo distress. Bravo jumped over the center console to ride with Mason. Aubrey decided not to take the dog's prefer-ence for his owner personally.

The way Bravo had warned her of danger was impressive.

"What happened?" Mason asked when they were far enough away from Nanette's apartment. "Did someone try to get in the car?"

She shook her head, flexing her fingers from their white-knuckled grip. "I had the window open partway, and when he caught a whiff of the three men coming toward us, he went nuts. I'm pretty sure they were all armed, and when one of them reached for their gun, I decided to get out of there." She met his gaze in the rearview. "I was worried about leaving you behind, though, so I drove toward Nanette's apartment. I'm really glad we found you."

"You did the right thing," Mason said. He smiled at his K9 and rubbed his fur. "Good boy. You protected her exactly the way I asked you too."

"But I almost left you behind!" Now that the danger was over, her eyes filled with tears. She swiped them away, irrationally angry with him. "We need a better plan, Mason. A meeting point of some sort."

"I would have called you," he said reasonably. "And I can take care of myself."

"Against three men with guns?"

"Yes. But I'm sorry you were worried."

The apology wasn't necessary, but somehow it managed to soothe her anger. Retired SEALs were not bulletproof. Or knife proof.

"What do you know of Lucas's father?" Mason's question caught her off guard.

"I—think Nanette told me he died shortly after Lucas was born." She met his gaze. "Why do you ask?"

"Are you sure he's dead?" Mason's tone held a note of disappointment. "I found a photograph in her bedroom of the three of them. She was holding Lucas as a baby in her arms, standing beside a tall Hispanic man. I thought maybe Lucas's disappearing could be some sort of custody battle."

"Doubtful. For one thing, Nanette and Lucas didn't have any money to spare. If Lucas's father was alive, she'd be getting some sort of child support. I got the impression she was on her own, working as many hours as possible."

"Not all fathers support their kids," Mason pointed out.

"I know." She thought back to the brief conversation

she'd had with Nanette. "I asked about Lucas's father, and I'm sure she said he was dead."

Mason grimaced. "Okay, so finding the photograph wasn't a good lead after all."

She tried not to be depressed. Facing danger at every turn to come up with nothing was frustrating. Frankly, she wasn't impressed with the police work that had been done on this case so far, yet if this was what detective work was like, she was surprised they managed to arrest anyone at all.

"I found two coasters, one from Twisted and another from The Overlook. We should head there next."

Every cell in her body revolted at the thought of facing more danger. "Tonight?"

"Yeah." He looked at her oddly. "Most bars and taverns aren't open in the morning. Besides, how else are we going to find out the real name of *el jefe*."

"Okay." What else could she say? Mason was searching for Lucas because of her. He was putting himself in harm's way to find a missing boy only because she'd asked him to. Pretty hypocritical on her part to complain about his taking her concerns seriously. "I—don't know where it is."

"I'm looking it up." Mason stared at his phone. "Interestingly, it's not far from Twisted. I hope that means it's another Blue Devils hangout. Take a right up ahead. Go three blocks past Twisted, then hang a left."

She followed his directions. "I'll drive by the place first, then we can find a place to park."

"You read my mind." Mason flashed a quick grin. "That's exactly what I would have asked you to do."

His good mood didn't make her feel any better. No doubt he was trying to lighten things up because of the recent danger.

Yeah, it wasn't working. If anything, her stomach was tied in so many knots she wanted to double over in pain.

The Overlook appeared to be the same sort of establishment as Twisted. Maybe a slight step up, but not by much. What the place overlooked was a mystery as they were still too far from the ocean for a scenic view.

After driving past, she pulled over to the side of the road and turned in her seat to look at Mason. "We need a meeting spot in case something bad happens again. I can't bear the thought of leaving you behind."

"You did exactly the right thing back there, Aubrey." His gaze was serious. "I need you to trust in me and my skills."

"I do," she hastened to reassure him. "But you're not bulletproof either."

"No, but I'm much smarter than your average guy." The corner of his mouth quirked in a half smile. "Give me some credit."

"A meeting place," she repeated. "Pick one."

He was silent for a long moment. "The east entrance of Petco Park."

"The park?" She frowned. "That's pretty far away considering you're on foot."

"Heading to the Stanley School for the Deaf is too obvious. And the park is closer and in the opposite direction from my house." He gave Bravo another rub. "If Bravo alerts you to danger, get out of here. If he doesn't, give me twenty minutes. If I'm not back by then, go to the park's east entrance and give me another fifteen minutes."

That didn't seem to be nearly enough time. "And if you still don't show up?"

He shrugged. "Call the police and go back to my place." He reached up to rest his hand on her shoulder. "Sometimes it takes time to extricate from a dicey situation. Have faith, Aubrey."

"I do have faith," she said quickly. "I believe God is guiding us on this journey and that He is watching over us. But I want you to know I hate the thought of you being in danger. The police should be doing this."

"The guys at Twisted very quickly decided I was a cop and tried to get rid of me. I'm not a cop, but there's no way Russo or Lee would get anywhere if they went in to ask questions. They'd be made as detectives in a heartbeat."

Logically, she knew Mason was right. Yet she still didn't like it. Not one bit. She forced herself to nod in agreement. "Twenty minutes, followed by another fifteen," she repeated. "East entrance to Petco Park. And, Mason?"

He paused in the act of reaching for the door handle, arching his brow. "Yeah?"

"Go with God and come back to me." That sounded more personal than she'd intended, but she didn't care.

She wanted, *needed* Mason to return to her unscathed. Sending him out into danger like this was eating away at her.

"I will do everything in my power to do just that," he assured her. It wasn't a direct promise, but she'd take it.

Mason was the strongest and most courageous man she'd ever met. And as she watched him slip out of the SUV, leaving Bravo behind with the command to guard, she knew she was more than a little emotionally involved with the handsome SEAL.

Dear Lord, please keep Mason safe in Your care!

MASON WAS TOUCHED by Aubrey's concern. He could tell all this was weighing on her, yet Lucas was still out there, somewhere. He forced himself to strip Aubrey from his mind to focus on his mission. Since his last foray into Nanette's apartment hadn't yielded much intel, he needed this bar to provide something for them to go on.

They were fast running out of leads. Yet, they'd made some progress, more than Russo and Lee, that's for sure.

Staying in the shadows, he glanced down at Raymond Nassar's mug shot, then slid the device into his pocket. Maybe the guy was inside.

Like earlier, he did a quick survey of the buildings around the tavern, identifying various escape strategies. No fire escapes here, but the windows also weren't boarded up, so he figured he could always climb up if necessary. When he'd finished his surveillance, taking special note of the rear entrance to The Overlook, he flipped up the collar of his jacket and hunched his shoulders. Unfortunately, there was nothing he could do about his military-style haircut. Normally, if he was going undercover, he'd dress the part.

But time was of the essence. They'd been at this all day and still weren't close to finding Lucas.

With every minute that passed, their chances of finding the boy alive and well dropped exponentially. Armed with his Sig Sauer, his knife, and steely determination, he stepped inside.

The place was just as busy as Twisted had been. He wasn't a fan of wall-to-wall people, but he squeezed past several patrons while subtly searching for a familiar face, like Nassar, Jose, or even the guys he mixed up with earlier.

He noted two men with Blue Devils tattoos. It never ceased to amaze him that these yahoos so obviously bragged about their gang status. Maybe it was a deterrent to some who'd rather not tangle with the gang, but it was also a beacon for every cop.

Making his way toward the rear exit, he caught a glimpse of a familiar face. Raymond Nassar in the flesh. Good. He was glad he'd found him. He briefly considered calling Russo but decided to hold off for a moment. Mason wanted to talk to the guy first without the cops hauling him off in cuffs.

Deep down, he wasn't convinced Nassar knew anything about Lucas. But he should know about the Blue Devils, maybe even the identity of the man in charge. Mason purposefully bumped into Nassar with enough force to spill the guy's drink.

"Oh, hey man, sorry," he said, adding a fake slur. Mason fumbled to pat the wet spot on the front of Nassar's shirt. "Ya wanna new one? Lemme buy ya one . . ." He looked around in confusion as if not knowing which way the bar was located.

"Stop it." Nassar swatted his hand away. "Get away from me."

Mason blinked and peered at him. The noise level inside the bar made it difficult to hear, but he could guess by Nassar's expression he wasn't happy. "Hey, don't be mad, I'll buy ya a new one." He swayed, then purposefully stepped on the guy's foot, hard.

"You idiot!" Nassar pushed him away, but the crowded bar meant he didn't go far. Mason hid a smile as he bounced off the guy behind him and moved forward, pushing up against Nassar.

"You want—outside?" Nassar threatened.

"Why not?" Mason only caught part of his question but got the gist. He continued to act inebriated as getting Nassar outside was exactly what he wanted. "You need an attitude adjustment, dude." He ran all the words together as he shoved Nassar.

As expected, Nassar grabbed his arms and hauled him toward the rear exit. Mason stumbled over someone's foot, which played into his role. The only problem now was that he couldn't hear what Nassar or anyone else was saying. He hoped no one had recognized him from Twisted.

Nassar dragged him through the door and into the alley. Mason swiftly straightened and spun out of his grip, changing roles so that he was holding on to Nassar. He pressed the guy against the wall, keeping his right ear cocked toward him to hear better. "Where can I find *el jefe*?"

"You—aren't drunk!"

Mason barely refrained from rolling his eyes. He'd decided to try asking where to find the boss rather than focusing on his name. A possible location was better in the long run. "I'm tired of waiting for him to let me join the *Diablos Azules*," he continued. "I've done everything they've asked of me."

"Then you should know better than to confront *El Jefe*," Nassar whined. "He'll kill you, and anyone who talks."

"Like Jose?" Mason was weary of trying to be nice. He tightened his grip on Nassar. "Listen, with one call I can have the cops here, arresting you. Just tell me where to find *el jefe*, and I'll walk away. Your choice but make it fast."

"You're a cop?" Nassar sounded surprised.

"I only care about the boy, Lucas." Mason kept a wary eye on the exit. Most of the people around them had assumed he was drunk, but that didn't mean they wouldn't be coming to investigate sooner rather than later. "*El Jefe* snatched him, and I want him back." He pulled his Sig and pressed it to the base of Nassar's skull, right above the Blue Devils tattoo. "Where is he?"

"Cops can't kill people," Nassar protested.

"I'm not a cop. But I am the man who will take *el jefe* down if he hurt Lucas in any way. And if the boss man is gone, you'll have nothing to worry about, right?" He leaned in. "You have one more chance, Nassar. Talk or die." Mason prayed Nassar wouldn't call his bluff. The worst he could do was haul the wanted man farther away from the tavern and turn him over to the police.

"He lives in Ratland—" Nassar abruptly cut off what he was saying as the rear door of the tavern opened.

Mason threw Nassar toward the two men standing there, staring in shock. Then he kicked it into high gear, running along the building in a zigzag pattern before disappearing around the corner.

He pulled out his phone and dialed 911. "Raymond Nassar is outside The Overlook in East Village."

He didn't wait for the dispatcher to acknowledge him but continued on his path away from the tavern. When he turned the next corner, he saw the SUV up ahead.

While he was glad he didn't have to leap tall buildings this time, he was a little concerned about these guys being on his tail. No gunfire yet, but he couldn't trust his ability to hear their footsteps pounding on the pavement behind him.

Aubrey flashed the headlights. He decided to take that as a good sign. Sprinting the last few yards, he was reaching for the door when the sound of gunfire rang out.

Man, being shot at by a bunch of Blue Devils was getting old.

He swallowed a curse and dove into the SUV. Aubrey took off without waiting for him to close the door behind him. To her credit, she peeled away from the curb and shot down the street like a pro race car driver. More gunfire echoed as she took the corner.

This time, the rear window of the SUV cracked from the impact. Those morons had managed to hit his vehicle! He turned in his seat and took aim, intending to return fire.

"Stay down!" Aubrey screamed so loud, a dead man could have heard her.

"Keep going," he shouted back, keeping his gaze on the cracked rear window. The bullet had gone through the glass, but thankfully, the cracks were small enough that he could still see the area behind them.

The two men were hot on their tail, moving faster than Mason would have anticipated. One of them lifted their gun.

"Turn fast!" Mason shouted.

Aubrey cranked the wheel so that she was driving on the wrong side of the road. The maneuver worked as the bullet didn't hit them.

"Good job," he called out. The guys on the street were smaller now as Aubrey kept going.

She turned at the next intersection, and the men disappeared from his line of sight. Still, he didn't move until she'd gone far enough that there was no possible way the two men could have followed them.

Not on foot. But he knew there was a possibility they may have had a car nearby.

He glanced back at Aubrey and Bravo. This time, for some reason, the dog had stayed up front beside her. Maybe instinctively knowing the danger was higher in the back seat.

"Good boy, Bravo." He met Aubrey's gaze. "And you did a great job getting us away from there."

"I'm getting lots of practice," she said dryly. Thankfully,

she didn't look like she was about to throw up as she had earlier.

It was disturbing to realize Aubrey was growing accustomed to being in danger. To being shot at by gang members.

"Who did you make mad this time?" she asked wearily.

He turned to sit, offering a wry grin. "Found Raymond Nassar. He told me *el jefe* is located in Ratland, wherever that is."

"Ratland?" She scowled. "That makes no sense. There's no town called Ratland anywhere in San Diego."

"I know." He lifted his arm, then winced in pain. Glancing at his right arm, his nondominant one, he realized the bullet that had gone through the window had grazed him. He rolled up his sleeve to examine the wound.

"Are you hit?" Aubrey's voice reeked of panic. "I'll drive you to the closest hospital."

"I'm fine, it's just a flesh wound." It hurt but not bad enough to require medical care. "I have a first aid kit at home."

"A first aid kit for a bullet wound?" Her tone was even more frantic now as if the reality of his close call was just sinking in.

"Aubrey, look at me." He reached up with his right hand to clasp her shoulder. "Please trust what I'm telling you. I'm fine. This is nothing more serious than a flesh wound. There's nothing to do except to clean it and wrap it in gauze. Okay?"

"O—kay." Her voice had calmed a bit, for which he was grateful.

"Do you know how to get to my place?"

She gave a curt nod without saying anything more. Bravo decided to come back to join him, so he gave the K9 a rub and then gave him the hand signal for down. Bravo curled up in the seat beside him.

Fifteen minutes later, Aubrey pulled into his driveway. He'd used one of Bravo's towels to wrap his injured arm, and she blanched when she saw him cradling it to his chest.

"Just a flesh wound?" she challenged.

"I promise." He was only holding the arm to keep the towel in place. "Come inside, you'll see for yourself."

She took his key, opened the front door, and waited for Bravo to trot in first. Mason gestured for Aubrey to wait inside the foyer as he and Bravo went through the house. It was a habit more than anything, he didn't really think any of the Blue Devils knew where he lived or had the resources to get that information.

Once the house was clear, he drew Aubrey in, closing and locking the door behind her. He followed her into the kitchen. "Have a seat. I'll get the first aid kit."

She sank into a chair, watching him warily. Bravo stretched out at her feet. He gave the K9 the hand signal for stay, then fetched the first aid kit from his master bathroom.

The first aid kit was larger than most, filled with just about anything a SEAL might need. Again, old habits died hard, but he was glad to have supplies.

When he returned to the kitchen, Aubrey looked up at him wearily. "You should know that I'm not very good with blood."

He chuckled. She scowled. "That's not funny."

"Yeah, it kinda is." He shook his head. "I can clean it myself."

"No, I'll help." She squared her shoulders, stood, and began rooting through his cupboards. "We'll start with warm soapy water."

He wasn't sure why her attitude amused him. Maybe it

was a reaction to the day's events. Or maybe he was just losing his mind. Either way, he enjoyed Aubrey's company, even though he hadn't spent this much time with a woman in what seemed like forever.

She spread a dishtowel on the table, then gestured to the chair. "Sit down. Let's take a look."

He sat and unwrapped the towel. Then he stripped off his shirt so that she could see his arm. The gash was jagged, blood oozing from the wound, but thankfully, it wasn't deep.

Aubrey paled, then dropped her gaze to the washcloth in her hand. With sheer determination, she gently cleaned the wound.

"Told you it wasn't bad," he said.

She covered the wound and glanced up at him. "It pains me to see you injured, Mason."

Her words touched him deep in the recesses of a heart he didn't think he had. "I'm sorry to worry you," he managed.

She finished cleaning the wound, then placed a few squares of gauze over the wound before wrapping a long roll of the stuff around his bicep to keep them in place. When she finished, she sank into a chair and put her head down between her knees.

"Aubrey?" He looked at her with concern. "Are you okay?"

She didn't answer. The next thing he knew, she'd passed out on the floor.

CHAPTER NINE

Aubrey blinked and looked up into Mason's concerned gaze. His face was so close she wouldn't have to move much at all to kiss him. Then she realized he was holding her in his arms, carrying her toward the sofa. Her cheeks flushed as she realized she'd fainted like some goofy damsel in distress.

How embarrassing.

Yet it had been like that for the past ten years, ever since she'd suffered the miscarriage of her son. Still, she had hoped to have gotten over this ridiculousness by now.

Apparently not.

"Aubrey? Are you okay?" Mason sat on the sofa, still cradling her against his chest. His concerned tone washed over her, making her realize just how long it had been since a man had held her. Cared about her.

"Yes, sorry." She struggled to sit up, but he held her in place. Bravo came and licked her arm. She couldn't help but smile. "I told you I'm not good with blood."

"Yeah, but you managed to bandage my wound before passing out, which was impressive."

"There's nothing impressive about ending up on the floor." She gazed up at him.

"Does this happen when your kids get hurt at school?" He seemed genuinely curious about the phenomenon.

"Not very much, and we have a nurse on duty who handles most things." She hesitated, then added, "It's more of an emotional thing for me. I—lost my eighteen-week-old son in a miscarriage three months before my husband passed away. Seeing his lifeless body amidst the blood . . ." She couldn't finish. The memory would haunt her for the rest of her life.

"I'm so sorry to hear that." Mason's low voice held empathy more so than pity. "I can't imagine how difficult that must have been for you."

She nodded, then moved again to sit up. This time, he shifted her so that she was beside him on the sofa rather than on his lap. "Thanks. I was hoping I'd gotten over it by now. Sorry about that."

"You have nothing to apologize for." His intense blue gaze seemed to look all the way into her soul. She liked that about him. That he paid attention when she spoke and never looked down at her for being out of shape and less than helpful when it came to dangerous situations. "I could have handled the wound myself. It wouldn't have been the first time."

She didn't doubt it. "I hope carrying me didn't make it bleed again."

"Nah. You did a great job in patching me up." His brow furrowed. "Losing your son and your husband so close together must have been terrible. Yet you still believe in God."

"Yes, well, don't think I wasn't mad at Him for several months, because I was." She raked her hand through her hair. "But in the end, I needed His solace. His grace. And no matter how much I pushed God away, He was there for me when I needed Him. When the loss of my family really hit hard." She waved a hand. "It took a while, you know? For weeks, I walked around in a daze as if Carter was on a business trip rather than gone. And I found some solace in knowing he was in a better place, without feeling any pain, with God."

"Your faith is powerful and amazing." He paused, then added, "My team lost a man during our last mission. The same mission that caused the complete hearing loss in my left ear. It's been hard for me to let go of the guilt I feel in Jaydon's death."

She rested her palm against his cheek. "You're not responsible for what happened, Mason. Don't you realize that God is ultimately in control? God knows when we were born and when we'll die."

"I was the team leader." A note of steel lined his tone. "My men were my responsibility."

"God gave you the strength and courage to lead your men," she agreed. "And as difficult as it is to understand, everything that happens is God's will. That was the hardest part for me to wrap my head around. Why did God need to take Carter and Noah from me so quickly? I was so angry, but eventually I let go of my resentment and accepted that this life I have is the one God has chosen for me. You need to accept that too, Mason."

He didn't say anything for a long moment. "That's a lot to ask."

"I know. Trust me, I've been there." She wished she could find a way to convince Mason to put aside his guilt. "God gave up His only son to save us. That was a lot to give up too. And consider this, Mason. Your loss and mine are what brought us together. Maybe God's plan is for us to find Lucas, to save another child's life."

"Yeah, maybe." She could tell the thought intrigued him. The fact that he didn't toss her words back in her face was a step in the right direction. "Are you hungry? I was planning to toss a pizza in the oven for dinner. Or we can order out if you'd rather have something else."

"Pizza sounds great." She was emotionally and physically exhausted, but her stomach rumbled with hunger. Must be all the excitement of the day catching up with her. "I'll set the table."

Mason stood and held out his hand. When she took it, tiny bolts of electricity zinged up her arm. She did her best to ignore the sensation that was thrilling and annoying at the same time. This wasn't the time or the place to think about starting up a relationship she didn't want. Yet there was no denying how drawn she was to him and how he made her feel attractive, even though she wasn't young or beautiful.

Carter had always called her cute as he kissed her upturned nose. She'd never doubted his love for her.

Yet somehow, Mason made her feel different. As if he found her beautiful, not that he'd said those words. And why did that make her feel guilty? Carter was gone and would never begrudge her happiness.

Mason dropped her hand and headed into the kitchen. "Plates and glasses are up here." He gestured toward the cupboard. She shook off the confusing thoughts and crossed over to join him. After fetching the plates and glasses, she opened drawers to find the silverware.

"Shouldn't we call the detectives?" She repacked the

first aid kit and set it aside. Mason had disposed of the bloody gauze and stained water.

"Probably." He didn't look enthusiastic about it. "I figure they'll call us once they hear about the gunfire."

"What about repairing the damage to the SUV?" She frowned. "I'll pay for that since it's my fault you're involved in this."

"No need, I'll handle it." Mason sighed and rubbed the back of his neck. "Now that I think about it, the slug is probably inside the vehicle. The detectives will want it as evidence. I will have to call them after we eat."

"Okay." She could already imagine how the conversation would go. It would be just like the last couple of times. They'd ask questions about what happened and then take the information they'd gathered. The one-way process was getting old.

Just once, it would be nice if they'd come with some information of their own. Finding Lucas was their job. Yet other than giving them the name of a Blue Devil, they'd been falling way short.

"Do you think they're holding back on us?"

Mason joined her at the table. "I've considered that possibility, but Russo in particular seemed willing to work with us on this."

She wrinkled her nose. "Yeah, I wish I could believe that."

A reluctant smile tugged at his mouth. "I hear you." The timer went off. He removed the pizza, cut it into slices, and set it in the center of the table.

Aubrey took Mason's hand again. "Lord, we ask you to bless this food, bless this house, and continue protecting us as we search for Lucas. Amen."

"Amen," Mason said. He held her hand for a long moment before letting go.

She felt herself blush as he set a slice of pizza on her plate. This intense awareness of Mason wasn't going anywhere, so she decided to accept it. For long moments, they were too busy eating to talk. Yet Aubrey found the silence comfortable rather than awkward. Since first coming here last night, much had changed between them. These past twenty-four hours with Mason made it seem as if they'd known each other for months rather than hours. She'd told him things she hadn't spoken of in years.

From this point forward, she knew he'd never just be another adult student learning sign language.

He was so much more.

She reminded herself not to fall for this man. They were together now because of a shared goal. A shared mission. Once Lucas was found, they'd go back to their usual routines. She sensed Mason was a bit of a loner, except for his SEAL team members. She wasn't under any illusions that he'd suddenly be interested in her as a woman.

Especially after her face-plant on the floor.

He'd been patient and kind about her shortcomings. Never once making her feel like she was holding him back, although she knew she was.

The ringing of a doorbell interrupted her train of thought. She glanced at Mason, who must have heard it too. He'd also probably noticed Bravo come out from beneath the table to stare toward the door.

He pulled his weapon and cautiously approached the door. Moments later, he relaxed. "Guess the news of the gunfire made it to Russo and Lee."

She finished her last bite of pizza, then rose and carried her plate to the sink. Mason still had a full slice of pizza on his plate, and she was irritated these guys had shown up before he'd had a chance to finish his meal.

"Ms. Clark," Detective Russo greeted her with a nod. "The officers in East Village took a report about someone seeing Raymond Nassar followed by gunfire taking place not far from a place called The Overlook. When we heard an SUV with two people were involved, we decided to swing by. The bullet hole in the back window of the SUV parked in the driveway confirmed our suspicions that you were involved."

"We were planning to call you after dinner." She looked pointedly at Mason's unfinished pizza. "And you may want to call your crime scene techs as we're sure the bullet is still inside the SUV."

The two detectives glanced at each other. "Mind if we head outside to take a look?" Lee asked Mason.

"Go ahead." Mason returned to pick up his remaining slice of pizza. "Don't mind me while I finish eating."

Bravo stood guard near the door as they headed back outside. Mason ate quickly, then wiped his mouth with a napkin. "I'm somewhat reassured that they came to check on us."

"You are?" She frowned. "Seems to me they're always late to the party."

"Yeah, well, better late than never." He carried his plate to the sink. "You can wait here. I'll head out to fill them in."

"I'm coming with you." She wanted to hear what, if anything, they'd discovered while she and Mason were dodging bullets.

Probably nothing, she thought sourly.

"The crime scene tech is on the way," Russo said as they joined them near the SUV. "From what I can tell, the bullet is lodged in the front passenger seat."

Where Bravo was sitting. She glanced at Mason in time to see him scowl. "Yeah, that's what I thought too. Bullet creased my arm, and there's an entry hole but no exit."

"Maybe you should stay out of this for a while," Lee suggested. She was glad his previous annoyance seemed to have faded a bit. "You keep kicking the sleeping bear, and it's only a matter of time before you get bit. I don't want to see either of you get hurt or worse by these guys."

Mason shrugged. "I'm fine. But tell me this, if you knew The Overlook was a place the Blue Devils tended to go, why not stake the place out?"

"We didn't know that until today when you made the call about seeing Nassar inside," Russo explained. "What happened?"

"I found Nassar, pretended to be drunk to get him outside. We chatted until a few more of his buddies showed up, forcing me to get out."

"Is that when they started shooting at you?" Russo asked.

"Not until I got into the SUV. Aubrey drove away just as they opened fire." He scowled and crossed his arms across his chest. "Good thing they don't have good aim."

She wanted to point out that their aim was good enough to pierce the rear window and wound him, but she held her tongue. She knew the entire situation could have turned out much worse.

Thankfully, God was watching over them.

"Did you learn anything about where Lucas is? Or who *el jefe* is?" Lee asked.

"Did you?" Aubrey shot back. "Why are we doing all the work on this case? What did you do all day?"

Mason reached out to put a calming hand on her arm. She wasn't in the mood to be calm. She was tired of this. Of worrying about what awful things were being done to Lucas while the police moved at a snail's pace. Of being shot at every single time they followed up on a lead.

She was truly torn between telling Mason to give up the search and pressing forward.

Dear Lord, show me the way . . .

MASON WANTED to grin at Aubrey's sassy attitude but did his best to cover his reaction. He'd admired her before, but the longer they worked together, the more he realized she had a heart of gold and a spine of steel.

Until she saw blood. Then again, hearing about the tragic loss of her son, he couldn't blame her one bit for her reaction.

"You have a right to be upset," Russo said. "So far we've questioned everyone in the neighborhood and found two people who saw Lucas Tuesday morning, heading to school. Since he never made it, we believe that's when he was taken. One person in the apartment building described a man who matches Jose, but we haven't gotten his last name yet."

"We did get some information from one of the Blue Devils inmates," Lee said. "Seems everyone is scared to death of *el jefe*. We've heard his headquarters is in Tijuana or in El Cajon."

"Those two cities are not exactly close together," Mason drawled.

"I know," Russo agreed, "which is why we can't be sure either location is accurate."

"Both of them are at least twenty minutes from East

Village and in opposite directions," Aubrey pointed out. "That seems wrong. I'm sure he must be close by."

"We plan to keep looking and asking questions. The good news is that our guys picked up Raymond Nassar." Russo glanced at Mason. "Thanks to your call."

"Where?" she demanded. "Why weren't your cops closer when his friends shot at us?"

"He ran toward Petco Park, which is where our guys scooped him up." Lee shrugged. "They heard the gunfire, but by the time they arrived, you two were long gone."

"Can you convince Nassar to talk?" Mason asked.

"That's the plan." Lee glanced back at the SUV. "Sounds like he wasn't one of the shooters this time, though."

"No, but he was in the stolen vehicle, which should be enough to use as leverage to find out more about Jose and *el jefe.*" Mason drilled the detective with a narrow look. "If Nassar wasn't the shooter himself, then he was the driver."

"Exactly. He played a role either way. We'll let you know what we find out." Russo glanced toward the street when a boxy-shaped van pulled up. "There's the crime scene tech. He'll get the slug out of the seat cushion and send it in for testing. Maybe it will match with another crime."

"That reminds me." Mason reached into the SUV and removed two guns. "I forgot to give these to you before. I took one of these off Jose, the other from a Blue Devil outside Twisted earlier today. You may want to see if either weapon matches any evidence you have on file related to other gun crimes."

Lee scowled. "You forgot? Seriously?"

Mason shrugged. "A lot has happened today. Besides,

I'm the one giving you key evidence when you've given me squat."

"It's not our job to give you evidence," Lee protested hotly.

"Easy now, we're all on the same side here," Russo said in a consoling tone. "We all want to find Lucas as soon as possible."

The cynical expression on Aubrey's face mirrored his own thoughts. Yet he wished he had given them the weapons earlier. Not that he was convinced either gun would provide a direct link to finding Lucas.

Yet at this point, they couldn't ignore a single lead, no matter how slim.

"Anything else?" Russo asked as they moved away from the SUV to let the crime scene tech get inside.

"Yeah. What area of the city or state is known as Ratland?" Mason watched both detectives closely.

They frowned and looked at each other. "Maybe Anaheim?" Lee guessed. "You know, Disneyland? Some people say the giant rat is in charge, meaning Mickey Mouse."

It was a possibility that hadn't occurred to him. "That's over ninety miles away."

"I was thinking maybe the term meant Ranchero," Russo suggested. "The Ranchero area would be closer to the city of El Cajon, which is one of the lower income cities that is also predominantly Hispanic."

He flushed at the thought he'd heard wrong. Darn his hearing loss anyway. Although now that he thought about it, Russo was probably right. *El jefe* being in Ranchero seemed more likely than Anaheim.

As if sensing his turmoil, Aubrey came over to take his hand in hers. "We should check out both possibilities."

"No, Ranchero is probably right." He gave her hand a gentle squeeze. "Anaheim is too big of a tourist attraction to set up illegal activities there. Ranchero, specifically El Cajon, is much closer and a more likely target."

"Farther from Mexico, though," Lee added, "if the Blue Devils are moving drugs in from one of the cartels there."

"I know." His initial instinct was to go to Tijuana as that was well known to be a drug hub. Yet it was also heavily patrolled by the DEA and the border police. "I guess anything is possible. For all I know, he was giving me a load of bull."

"He who?" Russo asked.

"Raymond Nassar. That's about all I could get out of him before his buddies showed up." He eyed the detectives. "Maybe you can get more out of him, especially if he knows he's facing attempted murder charges."

"We'll see what we can do," Russo agreed. "Good work on your part, Gray."

Mason nodded, but it didn't feel like good work. It felt as if he was swimming in a murky sea without land in sight. It irked him to know that following up on every lead had put Aubrey in danger.

Maybe he needed to check in with Kaleb again. With some pressure, he could easily convince his teammate to head down to help.

"Found it." The crime scene tech came over holding a small evidence bag up for them to see the smushed slug inside.

"Looks small caliber," Russo said.

"Likely a .38 Special," Mason drawled. "Similar to the weapon I took off that guy outside Twisted."

"Maybe the Blue Devils buy them in bulk?" Lee's attempt at humor fell flat.

"Let's hope not," Russo said. He handed the bag back to the tech. "Send it through the system, see if you get any matches. Oh, and do the same with these guns." He handed over the pistols.

"Will do." The tech took the items over to his square van. Moments later, he was gone.

"I hate to ask again, but anything else?" Russo looked him in the eye. "Don't hold out on us, Gray."

"Back at you," he said before he could stop himself. "But no, that's all I have for you."

Russo and Lee waited a beat before nodding. "We'll be in touch sometime tomorrow," Lee said before they turned away.

"Detective?" Aubrey called.

Russo turned back toward her. "Yeah?"

"Please do your best to find Lucas." For a moment, she looked as if she might cry. "If he's really been gone since Tuesday morning, we're already three days behind. He could be in Mexico by now."

"I promise we are working every lead we have on this case," Russo said reassuringly. "I'm aware of the timeline."

She nodded without saying anything further.

Once Russo and Lee were gone, he urged Aubrey back inside. "We both need to get some sleep."

"I know." She shook her head. "But it's hard to rest when you know Lucas is in terrible danger."

"We're doing our best and so are the detectives." Mason wished there was more he could do too. Unfortunately, he was fresh out of ideas.

"You didn't mention searching Nanette's apartment."

"No, I didn't think it prudent to describe how I broke the law." He shrugged. "Thankfully, they didn't ask why I went to The Overlook."

"I think we should go to El Cajon."

He sighed. "We're not going anywhere tonight, it's too dangerous. Besides, what do you suggest? That we stroll up and ask the locals to take us to *el jefe*? We're going to be seen as outsiders. I doubt anyone will talk to us much less help us find the boss man in charge of the Blue Devils."

"We need Nanette. Maybe she'd be able to get through to them."

Mason didn't want to point out that Nanette could very likely be with the Blue Devils too. Maybe it was a case of joining the gang to get close to her son. "Let's get some sleep."

Aubrey nodded and turned away. He took Bravo outside to walk the perimeter of his house.

Darkness was never absolute in the city, not compared to the blackness he'd experienced in Afghanistan. Still, he checked the shadows to make sure no one was lurking nearby. He paused at the damaged SUV, wishing he could hide it in the garage. But he didn't want Aubrey's car out where it could be easily seen either.

He stayed outside for far longer than was necessary to give Aubrey time to use the bathroom and head to bed. Holding her in his arms earlier had made him realize how emotionally involved he was.

How much he cared about her.

Maybe once this was over and they'd found Lucas, they could get together as a normal couple. Have dinner, maybe watch a movie.

Things he hadn't done in what seemed like forever.

A movement on the opposite side of his enclosed pool caught his attention. He hadn't heard anything, but these days he couldn't count on his hearing. The Ratland versus Ranchero was proof of that.

He knelt beside Bravo, using his K9's senses to cue him to any threats. The Malinois perked his ears forward, lifted his nose to the air, then let out a series of staccato barks loud enough to wake the entire neighborhood.

There! The shadow moved, then broke into a run. "Get him," he shouted.

Bravo took off like a rocket, with Mason following close on his heels.

CHAPTER TEN

The sharp barks from Bravo made Aubrey freeze in alarm. From the past twenty-four hours, she knew the dog only barked when he alerted on Lucas's scent or when there was danger.

This sounded like danger.

She had already changed into her flannel pajamas, so she quickly stripped them off and put her clothes back on. Shoving her feet into her shoes, she tiptoed out of the bedroom and peered down the short hallway.

The barking had stopped, but there was no sign of Mason or Bravo. She knew if Mason was here, he'd tell her to stay inside, but she hated the idea of standing around doing nothing. Glancing down at her phone, she debated calling 911. A number she'd never called before until yesterday. Now it had become second nature.

She pressed the numbers, then hesitated. What would she say? That Bravo had barked and that meant danger? With a groan, she shoved the phone back into her pocket. She'd wait to make the call.

Moving through the house, she peered out one window,

then the next. There was no sign of either Mason or Bravo. Her belly knotted with tension, but she reminded herself that Mason had proved over and over again that he was more than capable of holding his own.

She blew out a breath and did her best to remain calm. It wasn't that she was afraid of being left alone.

But of what Mason and Bravo were facing out there.

San Diego was a safe place to live. A beautiful city on the ocean. When had that changed?

She wasn't naïve enough to believe there hadn't always been crime happening around her. No city was immune from that.

But it hadn't touched her personally, until now.

Aubrey continued moving around the house, from one window to the next, hoping to see Mason and Bravo. The minutes ticked by with excruciating slowness.

Finally, man and dog emerged from the shadows. She was so glad to see them tears pricked her eyes. She quickly wiped them away and tried not to look as worried as she'd felt when Mason unlocked the front door and stepped inside.

"What happened?" Her tone came out sharper than she intended. So much for not looking concerned. "I heard Bravo barking."

"We took off after a man hiding in the shadows." Mason rested his hand on Bravo's head. "We almost caught him, but there was a car waiting for him. He managed to get inside before we could stop him."

"Who was he? Did he look familiar?"

"No, and we only saw him from a distance." Mason frowned. "He was fast, I'll give him that. Normally, Bravo would have gotten him. I had to call Bravo back, or he would have jumped in the car with him."

"Good grief." She shivered. "I don't understand. Were they with the Blue Devils? And how did they find us?"

"I can't say for sure those guys are with the Blue Devils, but we can't take any chances. The only way they could have found my location is by tracking the license plate of the SUV." Mason gestured toward the bedrooms. "You need to pack your things. We'll have to find another place to stay."

"A hotel?"

"Yeah." He eyed her warily. "You okay with that?"

Yesterday she'd have refused such a thing, but Mason had proved himself to be a gentleman and a protector. She didn't believe he'd force the issue of going to a hotel if it wasn't necessary for her safety. "Yes, of course. I'll pack my stuff."

He nodded and followed her down the hall. Minutes later, they met in the kitchen.

"I'm afraid we'll have to take your car," he said. "The broken window of the SUV is too noticeable."

"That's fine." She forced a smile. "My car is too boring to get anyone's attention."

"Trust me, that's a good thing." Mason lightly touched her arm. "I'll grab Bravo's stuff out of my SUV and move it out of the way so you can back out of the garage, okay?"

"Got it." They'd done this last night, which seemed like a week ago or longer. Again, she second-guessed her decision to try and find Lucas. The danger was all too real, and Mason had already been wounded.

She wasn't sure they should keep investigating. What if something even worse happened the next time they headed out to meet with one of the Blue Devils? She believed God was watching over them, but the fact that they'd been found here at Mason's house was far from reassuring.

Yet turning her back on Lucas felt wrong. He was young, deaf, mute, and likely scared to death.

No, she could not give up searching for him.

And somehow she knew Mason wouldn't either.

Once they had the damaged SUV parked in the garage, Mason placed their overnight bags in the trunk of her Kia. With Bravo in the back seat, they headed off.

"Any particular hotel?" She glanced at him questioningly.

"Nothing too fancy considering we have Bravo." He glanced at her. "I hope you're not disappointed."

"I'll be fine," she assured him. She noticed he drove to the other side of the city, away from his neighborhood and hers while close to East Village. He drove up to the main entrance of a well-known budget chain motel. "Wait here, I'll be back soon."

"Okay." As Mason disappeared inside, she realized they'd be sharing a room, likely with two double beds. As if being in the same house wasn't bad enough.

Oh, she trusted Mason not to try anything, he wasn't the type.

It was her own willpower she needed to be concerned with. Her awareness of Mason was off the charts. And very unsettling. He tempted her more than any man had in a very long time.

Kissing him again was not an option.

He emerged from the motel, casting a gaze around the area, before sliding in behind the wheel. "I was able to get us adjoining rooms for the next two nights."

She was surprised he'd even asked about that. "Ah, great. Thanks."

"Trust me, you'll be glad, Bravo snores," he teased as he

drove around to the rooms along one side. "We're in rooms seven and eight."

She nodded and waited until he parked before pushing out of the car. He let Bravo out of the back seat, then came around to unlock both doors. "Here's your key." He handed her the one for room 7. "I hope you don't mind opening your side of the connecting doors."

"Of course not." She entered the room, ignoring the musty smell, and did as he'd asked. Moments later, he dropped her suitcase on the bed, then went into his own room. After he unlocked his side, Bravo came through the opening, sniffing curiously.

"I'll reimburse you for my room," she offered.

He waved it off. "Don't worry about that. I would like to come up with a plan for the morning."

"I'm open to ideas." She plopped down onto the edge of her bed, exhaustion catching up with her. "The only thing I can come up with is visiting El Cajon. Not that I think that will get us very far. As you pointed out, we can't very well ask around for the Blue Devils."

"Yeah, but it may be worth a try." He stood in the doorway as if wary of invading her space. "Maybe Russo and Lee will come up with something too. For now, try to get some sleep."

"I will." She managed a smile. "Good night, Mason."

"Good night. Come, Bravo." Dog and man disappeared into their room, leaving the connecting door slightly ajar.

Aubrey stood and donned her flannel pajamas. She desperately needed sleep, but as she stretched out beneath the covers, everything that had happened since early that morning, tumbled through her mind.

She pushed the images away and silently prayed, first

thanking God for watching out for them, then asking that He provide peace and badly needed sleep.

When she woke up, light was streaming in through the motel window. She blinked, realizing she hadn't slept that well in a long time. She heard a door close and watched as Mason and Bravo walked past the window.

Using the brief time alone, she quickly showered, changed, and blow-dried her hair. By the time Mason and Bravo returned, she was ready for whatever the day might bring.

Today was Friday, which meant Lucas had been missing for four days. A long time for a young boy to be in the hands of the Blue Devils. And what if they'd already taken him across the border? Their chances of rescuing him would be slim to none if that had happened.

She shook her head, reminding herself not to imagine the worst. It was seven o'clock in the morning, so she made a quick call to the principal at the Stanley School for the Deaf to let him know she wouldn't be in that day. She'd braced herself for an argument, but thankfully, the call went straight to his voice mail.

She didn't even want to imagine what would happen if they hadn't found Lucas by Monday.

Crossing to the connecting door, she lightly rapped on it. She waited, then realized Mason may not have heard her. "Mason?" She projected her teacher's voice through the opening. "Are you decent?"

"Yeah." A hint of amusement laced his tone. She peered into the room and saw he was feeding Bravo. He turned to smile at her. "Good morning."

"Good morning." Her cheeks heated, and she had to resist the urge to cover them with her hands. This electric awareness of him had to stop. She was almost thirty-nine, too old to act like some sort of teenager with a crush.

"I don't suppose you've heard from Russo or Lee?" She edged farther into the room.

"Not yet." Mason gestured to Bravo. "When he's finished eating, we'll grab breakfast."

"We can drive through a fast-food restaurant for a breakfast burrito on the way to El Cajon." Despite her emotions being all over the place about heading into more danger, she figured they may as well get started. The sooner they checked the city for any sign the Blue Devils were using it as their headquarters, the better.

Mason hesitated, then shook his head. "There's a family restaurant next door. We'll eat first so I can check in with Russo and Lee."

The way he avoided her gaze made her think he was planning to leave her behind. To her shame, there was a tiny part of her that wanted nothing more than to hide in the motel room.

But she wasn't going to do that. Mason needed backup, and while she might not be any good in a fight, she'd managed to call for help, twice, and to drive them to safety.

Surely that was better than nothing.

MAN, he wished Kaleb was with him. Or any of the guys, really. He would prefer to have backup while searching for Lucas.

Late last night, he'd decided against taking Aubrey to El Cajon. He felt certain she was safer here in the motel since he'd made sure no one had followed them. And despite the fact that they'd managed to find his place either by a chance sighting of his damaged SUV or through his license plate number, he didn't believe they had the resources to track his credit card.

He planned to hit the ATM for cash, anyway, so that they could stay completely off the radar from this point on.

First, though, he needed to follow up on the only lead they had. Upon reaching El Cajon, he planned to use Bravo's excellent nose to potentially pick up Lucas's scent. If the dog was able to do that, he'd know Lucas had been taken there at some point and could hopefully convince Russo and Lee to work with the local authorities to dig deeper into potential hiding spots.

Worrying about Aubrey would only slow him down.

She wouldn't like his decision. He mentally braced himself as they walked next door to the restaurant. He left Bravo in the motel room as he figured the dog would only attract unwanted attention.

The guy he and Bravo had chased last night might recognize the animal. Which was another reason he'd decided to head out to El Cajon.

And if Bravo didn't alert to Lucas's scent in the city, then they could scratch that location off the list.

Not that there weren't dozens of other possible locations they could be holding the boy. Many potentially located south of the border.

After the server brought coffee and took their order, Aubrey said, "Please don't go to El Cajon without me."

Scary the way she read him so easily. He took a sip from his mug. "You'll be safe at the motel, no one knows you're there."

"I haven't held you back so far," she pressed. "In fact, if I remember correctly, I was able to help you get out of several close calls."

"Yes, but that was because I had to come back to keep you safe." He eyed her over the rim of his mug. "I would have gotten away even if you weren't there. I always made sure to have at least two different escape routes."

She stared down at the table for a moment. "I hate holding you back." Her voice was so low he had to lean forward to hear her. She noticed his movement and lifted her head. "I keep thinking about what's better for Lucas. He knows me. If you find him, he'll feel better if I'm there to reassure him."

It was a difficult argument to ignore. "I know enough sign language to reassure him."

Aubrey reached across the table to take his hand. "If those men hurt him, he'll still be afraid of you, Mason."

He felt his resolve weakening. Good thing she wasn't asking for the sun and the stars as it was beginning to look like he was unable to deny her anything. He tried to find a compromise. "What if I find a motel where you can stay for a while that isn't too far from El Cajon? Will you wait for me there?"

She hesitated, and he could tell she didn't want to do that either.

"This entire trip could be a waste of time. I'm hopeful Bravo will alert on Lucas's scent, but if he doesn't? It's another dead end."

"Okay, I'll wait somewhere close by if you let me pay for the room."

It went against the grain to let her pay for anything, but he reminded himself that this was a compromise. "Sounds good."

Their meals arrived a moment later. He stared down at his eggs and bacon, remembering how Dawson had always prayed before eating a meal, even an MRE, which was basically fake mystery meat in a sealed pack.

Without thinking too much about his motives, he prayed for God to keep them safe as they continued searching for Lucas and to protect the boy from irreparable harm.

"Amen," Aubrey said.

He glanced up at her, belatedly realizing he must have whispered loud enough for her to overhear. "Amen," he agreed.

It didn't take long for them to finish their meals. He glanced frequently at his phone, but of course, he didn't hear from Russo or Lee.

Or Kaleb for that matter.

He paid the breakfast tab, then rose to his feet, holding his hand out to her. "Are you ready? Let's go."

After getting their bags from the motel and hitting an ATM for cash, he tried to call Russo, but the detective didn't answer. He left a message, explaining his plan to use Bravo to track Lucas's scent in El Cajon.

"I pray we find him today," Aubrey said as they hit the road.

"Me too." Mason glanced back at Bravo sprawled out on the back seat of the Kia. He didn't like driving without having the animal in a crate, but there wasn't another option at this point. Time was of the essence.

Five miles outside of El Cajon, he saw a motel similar to the one they'd just left. He pulled into the lot and glanced at Aubrey. "They'll probably charge extra since it's so early in the day. Why don't you let me get the room for you?"

"No need, I can manage." She slipped out of the car and hurried inside.

He hadn't seen anything unusual along the drive toward El Cajon, but he didn't relax his guard. He was already second-guessing his plan to leave her here when she returned. "I'm in room 104, and she didn't charge me extra at all. Sweet lady."

He lifted a brow. "That's great. Do you want your bag?"

"No, thanks." She paused, then added, "Please be careful."

"We will." He watched her disappear into the room, then drove away. Leaving her behind was difficult, but he knew his concentration would be much better now that he didn't have to worry about her being left alone and vulnerable in the car.

"We've got this, right, Bravo?"

The dog didn't answer.

Mason took his time driving through town. Easy to see the average income was much lower here than in San Diego, maybe even a little less than East Village. He scouted for large buildings that could be potential places for gang members to hang out or where *el jefe* may be living. He didn't think the boss man would show off his cash, more than likely he'd want to fit in with the rest of the citizens.

Flashing big money in this area would draw unwanted attention. And would cause others to suspect criminal activity. Very different from fighting the Taliban. The head honcho often had a very large and well-guarded house, boasting his position of authority. It was a form of intimidation to keep others in line.

There was one rather large yet dilapidated house that caught his attention. Another mile from there, he found a boarded-up two-story building. A restaurant that was clearly out of business appeared to have once occupied the first floor, with possible living space up above.

He found plenty of other ramshackle types of homes, too many to count. There were a couple of open bars and restaurants, a Mexican place, and what appeared to be a burger joint. He took note of the small grocery store and a couple of gas stations, one health clinic and one school that covered grades K–12. There was a sign that indicated they were hiring.

It seemed to him that most of the people who lived in the town also worked there. He and Bravo would be pegged as strangers from the get-go, with the news spreading through town faster than the speed of light, but he didn't see a way around that.

Good thing he'd left Aubrey at the motel.

After taking in the entire town, he plotted their course. He parked behind the boarded-up restaurant and let Bravo out of the car. He offered the scent bag containing Lucas's sweatshirt to his K9. "Seek! Seek Lucas!"

Bravo went to work, lifting his snout and taking in the scents around them. Then the Malinois lowered his nose and sniffed along the ground, making a zigzag pattern. He kept Bravo on leash because it was broad daylight and there could be kids around heading to school.

Bravo sniffed all the way around the entire abandoned building without alerting. Mason tried not to react to the dog in any way, placing his trust in the K9's ability. Keeping his tone level, he continued to encourage him. "Seek Lucas!"

The two-story dilapidated house was a couple of blocks away to the south. The most difficult part of working as a search team was not leading the animal where you wanted him to go. Mason needed Bravo to set the course.

Of course, Bravo headed east rather than toward the two-story house. Mason kept pace with the Malinois as he continued searching for Lucas's scent. He noticed an older Hispanic man watching them suspiciously from his front yard and knew that it wouldn't take long for one of the fine citizens to head over to question him.

Less than five minutes later, a tall Hispanic strode toward him. "Are you lost?"

"Nope." Mason raked his gaze over the guy, unable to tell from the baggy clothes if he was carrying. "Just looking around town."

"Why?"

The blunt question made Mason realize this wasn't a casual conversation. "I'm thinking of buying a place."

The guy snorted with laughter. "No one comes here looking to buy a place. People are leaving here for better jobs almost every day."

"And some people like the low-stress lifestyle," Mason said. Bravo was standing at attention, his ears perked forward as he stared at the stranger. "To each his own."

For a moment, the guy's gaze bounced between Mason and the dog. "We don't like strangers."

"Thanks for the warning." Mason gave him a nod and kept going. Bravo didn't want to turn his back on the guy because the dog saw him as a threat.

Finally, the guy moved off, but now Mason felt as if there were dozens of eyes boring into him as they walked. "Seek," he said to Bravo.

The animal stuck his nose in the air, then suddenly whirled around. Mason's pulse spiked as Bravo went south.

Without guiding the dog, Bravo eventually headed straight toward the dilapidated two-story house. As they drew closer, the dog's nose went to the ground. As the dog quickened his pace, Mason kept a wary gaze out for any threats. If they managed to get close to Lucas or *el jefe*, he felt certain there would be more than one man coming out to stop them.

To Mason's surprise, Bravo went past the two-story house. The dog had caught something of interest but didn't alert.

Across the street from the Mexican restaurant was an avocado-colored ranch home that didn't look any different from the rest from the outside, other than being bigger than most. The windows were all covered with blinds, which also seemed unusual at this time of the year. In the cooler months, most people left the blinds open allowing sunlight to provide warmth.

Two men emerged from the Mexican restaurant just as Bravo alerted on the sidewalk just in front of the avocado house.

"Good boy," he praised, keeping a wary eye on the two men. He didn't doubt that there were others inside, ready to back them up. He straightened, then faced them. "*Buenos dias*," he called as if he hadn't just found proof that Lucas had been here at some point.

The men didn't return his greeting. They separated a bit, putting several feet of distance between them as they walked toward him.

Mason had subtly taken off Bravo's leash when he'd praised the animal for finding Lucas's scent. He stuffed it into his back pocket so that both hands were free as the men came closer.

"What are you doing?" the one on the right demanded.

"Walking my dog." Both men were armed, but they hadn't drawn their weapons.

Yet.

They stopped six feet from him. Mason wasn't worried, he'd faced worse situations.

But he didn't really want to make enemies here. Not if there was a chance Lucas might still be nearby.

"You need to leave," the man on the left said. "You're not welcome here."

There was a time to fight and a time to retreat. Mason eyed them warily wondering which way this would go.

If these men attacked, he wasn't going to have a choice but to defend himself, and Bravo. He could only hope he wouldn't have to kill anyone.

CHAPTER ELEVEN

Aubrey wished she hadn't agreed to wait at the motel. As someone who normally worked full time, she decided daytime television was awful. She should have brought a book to read or something else to do.

The room was so small that pacing made her dizzy.

Finally, she dropped down onto the edge of the bed, closed her eyes, and prayed for patience and for God to watch over Mason and Bravo.

When she heard a car engine, she stood and moved to the window. Peering through the heavy drapes, she frowned when she recognized her white Kia sedan pulling into the motel parking lot.

They were back already? She hurried over to open the door. "I didn't expect you back so soon."

"Yeah, well, I wasn't given much choice." Mason came inside with Bravo at his heels.

"What do you mean?"

He sighed as he turned to face her. "I was told to get out of there by two armed men. I wasn't sure they would let me go, but they did. However, it's clear the town doesn't welcome strangers."

Her jaw dropped in surprise. "They came right out and said that to you?"

"Yep. And they were armed. I was too, but I didn't want to fight them if I didn't have to." He glanced at Bravo. "He alerted at the driveway of a green ranch house across the street and down one house from a Mexican restaurant. I think getting so close to that property is what caused those men to come out and confront me."

Her pulse quickened. "Bravo really alerted on Lucas's scent?"

Mason nodded. "But don't get your hopes up too high, I didn't have time to verify the alert. I was hoping to walk around the block to see if he alerted again."

Too late, she was already clinging to the flash of hope. "If Lucas is here, then we should be able to get the detectives to approach the house, right?"

"I'm not sure we should let them know yet." Mason glanced at her. "For one thing, I'm not sure Bravo's alert will be enough to get a search warrant for the place. Besides, I don't want to put the occupants of the house on notice that we suspect them. I don't think either of the men who approached me knew that Bravo was following Lucas's scent."

"Well, we can't just sit here doing nothing." She planted her hands on her hips. "If Lucas is in El Cajon, we need to get him out."

He lifted a hand. "I didn't say we weren't going to get Lucas out of here, but the fact is the town is small enough that they easily identified me as someone who didn't belong."

She stared at him. "You think *el jefe* owns the place? That he has spies on the lookout for the authorities?"

"Maybe. I was only gone ninety minutes." He shrugged and sat in the chair near the door. "It might be better to return after dark."

"But—that's hours from now." She hated whining, but he couldn't seriously think they could do nothing until dusk fell. "Maybe I should head into the city. A woman alone probably wouldn't be considered a threat."

"No way." His stern expression did not invite argument. "If the Blue Devils own the town, the way we suspect, then there's nothing to prevent them from kidnapping you."

She didn't want to be kidnapped either, but what choice did they have? The thought of Lucas being held against his will there was driving her crazy.

Mason's phone rang. "It's Russo." He put the call on speaker and held the phone in his hand between them. "Good morning, Detective. I hope you're calling with good news."

"Well, that depends on your version of good," Russo said dryly. "One of the weapons you gave us last night was matched to a murder that took place three months ago in East Village."

A murder? She stared incredulously at Mason. "Who was killed?"

"A guy by the name of Richard Bender." Russo paused for a moment. "Does his name sound familiar?"

"No," she said, wishing it did.

"Not to me either," Mason admitted. "Did you get any prints from the weapon?"

"You mean besides yours? Yeah, one other set. Guy by the name of Alberto Cummings."

Another name that meant nothing to her. She did her best to rein in her frustration. "Does that mean this Alberto guy has been arrested in the past?"

"Yes, he did one year in jail for selling drugs, released about six months ago. Hang on, I'll send his mug shot over. Let me know if you recognize him."

Mason's phone pinged, and he swiped at the screen to see the photo. The man didn't look familiar to her, but Mason nodded slowly. "Yeah, I recognize him. That's the tall guy who I grabbed and pulled outside when I visited Twisted. He's the same one who mentioned *el jefe* had taken Lucas."

"I assume Cummings had the Blue Devil tattoo on the back of his neck?" Russo asked.

"Yes," Mason admitted.

"We've issued an arrest warrant for Cummings," Russo said. "Once we have him in custody, we'll interrogate him further on what he knows about the guy in charge of the Blue Devils and ask specifically about Lucas."

"I don't think he knows much more than he told me," Mason said grimly. "The Blue Devils organization operates under a hierarchy, and Cummings isn't high enough within the organization to know his name. He claimed he got his information about *el jefe* wanting Lucas from Jose."

"Maybe not, but he can give us other names. At this point, we'll take what we can get. And pinning a murder rap on him may be enough to convince him to talk."

"I hope so." Aubrey said, noting by Mason's expression that he didn't necessarily agree with Russo's assessment.

"Where are you?" Russo asked in an abrupt change of subject. "I ran past your house before calling, but no one was home."

"We're driving around," Mason answered evasively before she could say anything. "If we find anything related to Lucas's disappearance, we'll let you know."

There was a brief pause. "You're in El Cajon, aren't you?"

"No," Mason said. Which technically was true. Their motel was located outside the city limits of El Cajon.

"Be careful," Russo said, then clicked off.

"I still think we should have told him what we know about Bravo finding Lucas's scent," she said stubbornly. "What if he can get a search warrant based on Bravo's alert? You didn't even ask him about the possibility."

"There will be a point when we need Russo and Lee's help to get Lucas, but not yet." Mason stood and paced the length of the room. "Give me a moment to think this through. There may be a way to get back into the city without raising suspicion."

She suppressed a sigh and waited. After a few minutes, he stopped his pacing and turned back to face her. "There's a help wanted sign at the school."

"There is?" She jumped to her feet. "I'll apply, see if they're willing to interview me right away."

"Okay, but you wouldn't normally show up in jeans, would you?" Mason asked. "And I'm not letting you go alone. We need to head back and change our clothes. Maybe I can do something to help disguise myself. We'll pretend to be a couple looking to relocate to El Cajon from East Village."

"Not a move most people would make," she felt compelled to point out.

"I know, maybe we'll use a different story, one about losing your husband and wanting to start over. I'll be your concerned brother." He offered a wry smile. "Sticking close to the truth is the best way to sound legit."

She nodded, even though Mason was hardly like a brother to her. Quite the opposite. "Okay. Let's do it."

"We'll rent a vehicle too," Mason said as they left the motel. "I'll drop my SUV off at the dealership and ask for a replacement."

Aubrey was relieved to have a plan. Mason drove to her place so she could change her clothes and get her teaching degree and resume. She wasn't worried about the task before her, until they returned to El Cajon. Nerves fluttered in her belly as Mason drove into the town from the opposite direction, hoping to avoid the Mexican restaurant and the men there.

She was wearing a sedate navy blue skirt and jacket paired with a white blouse. Low-heeled navy blue pumps gave her an extra inch of height, but she was still far shorter than Mason. While he'd arranged for the car, she'd gone online to find the application and to get the phone number. When she'd made the call about the teaching position, the woman on the other end of the line sounded pleased and readily agreed to set up an interview at one o'clock in the afternoon.

They arrived at the school early after leaving Bravo at the motel outside of El Cajon.

Mason accompanied her inside the school, which was also unnerving. She'd never in her life had a man accompany her to a job interview and felt certain it would look suspicious.

But she needn't have worried. Mason played his role well. "Good afternoon, my sister lost her husband recently and is looking to relocate here to start over. I hate to think of her being here alone. Are you aware of any other job opportunities that might be available? Maybe within the police department? I have law enforcement experience from San Diego."

"Not that I know of," the receptionist said, glancing between the two of them.

"He's being a bit overprotective," Aubrey said with a wry smile. "I'm sure I'll be fine on my own." She let her smile fade away. "Starting over in a new city should help."

"Gerry's Gas is always looking for help," the receptionist said with a smile. "The work isn't glamorous I'm afraid."

"I'll check it out, thanks." Mason turned to face her. "I'll swing by later to pick you up, sis. Good luck."

"Thanks." She kissed him on the cheek. "Now stop worrying about me."

Mason nodded and left her alone. She turned back toward the receptionist. "I'm really sorry about that."

"I think it's sweet that your brother is looking out for you." The woman stood. "Come on, I'll walk you over to Ms. Juniper's office."

She sat across from the principal, trying not to feel guilty about leading the woman on about a teaching position she had no intention of taking. It was for a good cause, finding Lucas trumped everything else, but lying didn't come easily.

As Ms. Juniper began to describe the school, she silently prayed for forgiveness.

WEARING A BALL CAP, clear glasses, and a fake mustache, Mason slid behind the wheel of the rental, a tan

SUV, and drove past the school toward the avocado-green ranch home. He'd scoured the real estate listings until he'd found one home for sale in El Cajon, not too far from where Bravo had alerted. He'd decided to pretend to be lost as he drove around the neighborhood.

The house was the second from the corner. He didn't so much as glance at the Mexican restaurant as he went past, acting as if he'd never been there before. He turned a few blocks down and continued going around until he was parked on the street behind the green house.

It wouldn't be easy to sneak around in broad daylight, but he carried a printout of the real estate listing in his hand, pretending to look at them as he reviewed house numbers. When he could see the back of the avocado house, he was glad to see the yellow house that backed up against it appeared to be deserted.

He approached the front door of the yellow house and knocked. No answer. He knocked again, looked down at his paperwork as if confused, then went along the side of the house until he was in the backyard.

Hiding near a scrubby bush, he raked his gaze over the rear side of the avocado ranch. One small window wasn't covered with blinds or drapes. Without giving himself a chance to second-guess himself, he darted across the two lawns until he was up against the side of the structure.

The small window likely belonged to one of the bedrooms, based on the customary layout of the typical ranch California home. Slinking along the rear of the house, he crept up to the window and did a quick turkey peek inside.

It was a bedroom, and he felt sure there was someone lying on the bed. He wanted to take a second look but first used his phone to snap a picture. Casting a glance around the area, to make sure no one was watching, he once again peered through the window.

Someone was lying on the bed, facing the wall. He was trying to judge if the size was too big to be Lucas when he felt the side of the house vibrate a bit as if a door had slammed shut.

Spinning away from the window, he quickly ran back toward the yellow house, where he slowed to a walk as he once more consulted his paperwork. Moving slowly, he headed down the street in the opposite direction from the green ranch to where he'd left his tan SUV. After sliding behind the wheel, he noticed movement up ahead.

Two men, not the same ones who confronted him earlier, had come out to stand on the street, looking around curiously. Mason debated whether to stay put or to drive away. Since these were not the same thugs he'd run into earlier, and he looked a bit different, he decided to start the SUV and to put it in gear.

He drove sedately, holding the paperwork up over the top of the steering wheel. He slowed near the men and rolled down his window. "Excuse me, can you help me find 1129 West Rolland Avenue? My sister is a teacher and is interviewing for a job at the school. There's a house for sale that she's interested in." He showed them the listing.

"It's about four blocks down from here," the younger of the two said. The older guy was frowning but didn't add anything to the conversation.

"Thanks." Mason lifted the window and turned in that direction. The men didn't follow or continue watching him. He blew out a sigh of relief when they turned and headed back the direction they came from.

The green house? Maybe. Or maybe another place close

by. If this was the headquarters of *el jefe*, he didn't doubt the boss man owned more than one property. He likely owned several of them.

Mason made sure to drive all the way to the house that was for sale before turning and heading back to the school. He parked in the lot and pulled out his phone.

The picture he'd taken through the window wasn't as clear as he'd have liked, but he could see the basic layout of the room, including the person lying on the bed facing the wall. He stared at it for a long moment but couldn't say for sure if the person was a small woman or a child.

Not a large man, that much he could tell. Yet Jose and some of the other men he'd met weren't that tall either.

His phone buzzed with an incoming text. Aubrey's interview was over. He messaged her back, saying he'd pick her up at the front door. By the time he'd backed out of his parking space and drove there, she was waiting.

"How did it go?" he asked when she settled in beside him.

"Too well. They offered me the job, and I felt compelled to tell them I had one more interview later today but that I'd let them know." She looked miserable. "I hated having to lie to them; it's clear they desperately need teachers."

"I know, and I'm sorry about that. But look at this." He handed over his phone with the picture he'd taken through the window up on the screen. "Tell me what you think."

"Is this Lucas?" she demanded.

"Do you recognize him as Lucas?" He shot her a glance. "Enough to swear to it in court if necessary?"

She bit her lip and continued looking at the photo. "I—no. I can't see his face."

That's what he'd been afraid of. "I can't either."

"Is this from the green house?" She continued looking from the phone to him. "How did you get so close?"

"Wasn't easy and I didn't get to stick around for long." He grimaced. "I'll come back later tonight, after dark."

"That's still hours from now," she repeated, reluctantly handing his phone back. "I wish I could see the person's face. Then I'd know for sure if that's Lucas or not."

"All I can make out is dark hair, but I can't tell if it's long or short." He set the phone in the cup holder between them. "Probably not enough to go to Russo and Lee for a search warrant either."

"I know." She sighed and put a hand on his arm. "I asked to see the fifth-grade classroom, since that's the grade I currently teach. They have fifth and sixth grades combined, and I checked out all the kids, hoping to see Lucas. But he wasn't there."

"Smart move." He liked the warmth of her hand on his arm. "Did you learn anything else helpful?"

"Just that most of the kids are Hispanic or white, not very many African Americans, which is different than what I see in San Diego." She lifted her hand to tuck her hair behind her ear. "It's obviously a very small community, one school for all twelve grades, which is why some of the grades are combined."

"Interesting that there aren't many houses for sale or other job openings," he noted. "Other than needing teachers, the place seems self-sufficient."

"On the surface, it seems like a nice place. But if *el jefe* owns half the town and is holding Lucas here . . ." Her voice trailed off.

He couldn't ignore the possibility that Bravo had given a false alert and that there may not be anything sinister about El Cajon.

Yet those men had come out of the Mexican restaurant to confront and warn him off for a reason. And there wasn't a doubt in his mind that the reason centered around illegal activity of some sort.

Not that the city appeared to be a hot bed of crime, at least not yet. He'd been in places where drug deals and prostitution took place in broad daylight where anyone could see.

He knew El Cajon had a small police department, and he found it curious they weren't looking for help. And he hadn't seen any officers out on patrol while he'd been there either. Not that he'd spent more than two hours in the area, but still.

It made him wonder if the police department was working for *el jefe*. A possibility he couldn't afford to ignore.

"Where are we going?" Aubrey asked.

"Back to the motel. I need to check on Bravo." There also wasn't anything else they could do in El Cajon until darkness fell.

"You're going back later, alone, aren't you?" Aubrey asked once they returned to the motel room.

"Yes. I hope to find out who that person is in the bedroom of the green house," he admitted. "If it's Lucas, we'll call for backup."

"Why not tell Russo and Lee ahead of time?" She looked upset. "Calling them when they're a good twenty minutes away isn't helpful."

"We don't know that it's Lucas. We don't even know that *el jefe* is in the area at all." He looked at the computer she'd brought from her place. "I wonder if there's a way to search property records, see who owns the green house."

"I can do that, if you know the address?"

"Yeah." He opened the laptop and turned it toward her.

She searched the El Cajon property listings. It didn't take long to find the address of the green house. "That figures," she muttered.

"What?"

"The owner is listed as a company rather than a person. Sunrise Investments, LLC."

That was interesting. "Can you search on that?"

"Yeah, but I'm not finding anything." As he watched, she went back to the property list. When she searched on Sunrise Investments, two more houses popped up on the screen.

He let out a low whistle. "They own several homes in El Cajon, which is really unusual." It made him wonder about the one house that was for sale. Was it going to be snatched up by Sunrise Investments too?

"You need to call Russo and Lee," Aubrey said. "Maybe they know something about the company."

As much as he didn't want to involve either detective yet, he slowly nodded. Pulling out his phone, he set it next to the computer and went to his recent call list to find Russo's name.

"Put it on speaker," Aubrey said.

He did so, and moments later, the detective picked up. "Russo."

"It's me and Aubrey. Did your officers pick up Alberto Cummings yet?"

"No. Are you still in El Cajon?" Russo asked.

"I have been searching on properties in the El Cajon area," he admitted. "I found one house for sale, but that's all. Which seems weird for a town that has a lower than average income per household. And I discovered several properties here are owned by a company."

"Oh yeah?" Russo sounded interested now. "What's the name?"

"Sunrise Investments, LLC." Mason waited a beat. "Does that ring a bell?"

"It sounds familiar, but I can't say how." Mason heard the clicking of computer keys in the background. "Let me do some digging and call you back."

"It's important," Mason stressed. "We found three houses owned by them so far. I think it's possible *el jefe* is the ultimate owner of Sunrise Investments, LLC."

"We need proof of that before we go storming the gates," Russo said curtly. "Give me some time, okay? I said I'll call you back."

"Okay, thanks." He hit the end button and met Aubrey's gaze. "We might be one step closer to finding Lucas."

"Oh, Mason, I hope so." She reached out to clasp his hand. "Let's pray we do."

He couldn't deny her anything, so he nodded and bowed his head. "Dear Lord, we need Your wisdom and guidance to find Lucas," he began.

"Please give us the strength and knowledge we need to save Lucas's life," Aubrey added. "Amen."

"Amen." He was surprised to feel a strange sense of peace wash over him.

The rest of the day passed by slowly. Normally, he had the patience of a saint, something drilled into him during his years in the navy, but not today. Not when he felt certain Lucas might be just a few miles away.

They grabbed a bite to eat from the fast-food joint nearby. Russo called back to say that he and Lee were heading to El Cajon. After Mason gave them the name of their hotel, Russo added, "Wait for us to get there before you do anything."

"Did you find something out about the investment company?" Mason asked.

"We'll fill you in soon." Russo promised and disconnected from the line.

Annoyed, he took Bravo outside for a bathroom break. Aubrey came with him, shivering in the cool night air. "What do you think they found?"

Twin headlights pulled into the motel parking lot. "Not sure, but it looks like we'll find out soon enough."

The detectives quickly joined them in the small room.

"Sunrise Investments owns Twisted," Lee said. "Now tell us what you know."

Mason explained about how Bravo alerted outside one of the houses owned by the LLC and showed them the photograph he'd taken through the bedroom window. "You can't see the face, so I can't say that Lucas is there."

The detectives glanced at each other. "I think that may be enough for us to knock on the door and ask questions," Russo said.

He suppressed a sigh and nodded. "Okay, but I'm going around back while you approach from the front, understand? And if I see Lucas, I'm going in."

"Sounds good," Lee agreed. "If you see the boy, that's enough for exigent circumstances."

The trip to the avocado-colored house didn't take long. Mason directed Aubrey to go around the back and to park a few yards down from the yellow house. He slipped out of the SUV and once again darted through the adjoining yards to sneak up on the back side of the green ranch.

He hurried over to the bedroom window and cupped his hands around his face to see inside. He went still when he realized the room was empty, the bed stripped bare as if no one had been there.

Mason swallowed hard. Whoever had been kept there must have been moved someplace else.

To a location they may never find.

CHAPTER TWELVE

It wasn't easy to wait in the car with Bravo, although she should be used to it by now. When she saw movement between two houses, she tensed, then relaxed when she realized Mason was standing there. He used sign language to tell her the bedroom was empty and that he was going around front to meet with the detectives. The news was disheartening, but she managed to respond with an okay sign. Then she quickly started the SUV and drove around to the front of the house.

Mason's expression was grim as he spoke with the detectives. She slid out from behind the wheel and quickly joined them.

"What happened?"

"Looks like they moved out," Russo said with a sigh.

"The windows were covered with blinds earlier, now they're all open, and you can see that there's nothing personal that's been left behind," Mason added. "We should have moved in earlier. Now we'll never know where to find Lucas."

"We don't know for sure Lucas was even here," Lee protested.

"Then why the hustle to leave?" Mason demanded. He rubbed the back of his neck. "I must have blown my cover earlier with those two guys. Maybe if I hadn't stopped to chat about the house that was for sale, they wouldn't have moved him."

Despite her despair over the news, she put her hand on his shoulder. "This isn't your fault, Mason."

"I should have broken into the house," he said, ignoring her. "Then we'd have Lucas safe."

"Hold on, you can't just break into houses because you suspect a missing kid is inside," Russo pointed out. "That's an unlawful entry."

"The rules don't matter when a kid is missing," Mason shot back. "Remember?"

"We can't condone breaking the law," Lee said.

"Stop it! Fighting among ourselves isn't helping," Aubrey snapped.

The three men looked at her in surprise.

"Is there a way to get inside the place to search for Lucas's fingerprints?" she asked, looking pointedly at the detectives. "What would you need for a search warrant?"

"I'll get Bravo." Mason spun toward the SUV.

"A photograph through a window isn't enough," Russo said. "Not even with the property owner being Sunrise Investments, LLC."

"Bravo alerted on Lucas's scent," she reminded them. "Surely all three things together would be enough."

"It's dicey because El Cajon is outside our jurisdiction," Lee said slowly.

"Seek! Seek Lucas!"

She turned to watch Mason and Bravo. The dog lifted his nose to the air, then trotted in a circular pattern before heading directly toward the driveway of the green house. Bravo sniffed the area near the edge of the driveway before promptly planting his butt and staring up at Mason expectantly.

"Lucas was here, likely taken out of the house and put in a car," Mason said as he rewarded Bravo for a job well done.

The detectives glanced at each other, then Russo nodded. "Okay, you've convinced me. Let me make a few calls, see if we can find a friendly judge." He lifted his phone and stepped away from them.

"I don't think I've ever seen a dog as well trained as Bravo," Lee admitted. "He's impressive."

"Yeah, he is." Mason glanced over to where Russo was speaking on the phone. "What are the chances we'll be granted permission to go inside?"

"I'm not sure we've ever used a trained dog scenting a kid as a reason to access a residence." Lee shrugged. "But Russo has some good connections. If anyone can get this accomplished, he can."

Aubrey appreciated Lee's change in attitude toward the case. She looked at the dark house, thinking about Mason's comment. If he had broken in earlier, they may have been able to save Lucas's life.

So close. Based on Bravo's alert, Lucas had been there. She firmly believed he must have been the figure Mason had seen through the bedroom window just a few hours earlier.

Now he was gone.

"Okay, we got the warrant," Russo said, returning to where they waited. "But we're supposed to notify the local cops so they can assist."

"And if the local cops are on *el jefe's* payroll?" Mason asked.

Russo shrugged. "We'll deal with that if it turns out they aren't being forthright with us."

"I'll call them in," Lee offered.

"Do we have to wait?" Aubrey pinned Russo with a knowing look. "Lee can make the call, but meanwhile, we should be able to go inside, right?"

"Lee and I can go inside," Russo corrected. "You'll have to wait."

"I'm not waiting. We can use Bravo to see if he alerts on Lucas's scent," Mason interjected. "And the sooner we do that, the better. Before the locals show up."

"They're sending a squad," Lee informed them.

"Good enough." Russo looked at the door. "It's locked, so we'll need to break in."

In answer, Mason lifted his booted foot and slammed it into the doorjamb. The wood splintered, and the door swung open.

Russo shook his head but pulled his weapon before stepping inside. "Police," he shouted. "We have a search warrant!"

There was no response. Aubrey watched as Lee followed Russo inside. Mason gave them a moment to clear the house before offering Bravo the scent bag again. "Seek! Seek Lucas!"

The dog nimbly entered the home. Aubrey followed them to the open doorway, not surprised when Bravo alerted in the kitchen. She waited for Bravo and Mason to return from the bedrooms.

"He alerted near the bed," Mason informed her. "I really wish I'd broken in when I had the chance."

While she knew Russo and Lee disagreed based on the

legal side of things, she found herself aligned with Mason on this. Rescuing Lucas had to be the top priority.

"We'd better wait outside," she said, glancing over her shoulder at the twin headlights piercing the darkness. "The local police have arrived."

Mason joined her near the rental. The officers who emerged from the squad were dressed in dark uniforms. "Detective Lee?" the shorter man asked.

"Detectives Russo and Lee are inside," Aubrey said helpfully. "Do you know who owns this place?"

The taller cop shot her a suspicious look. "No." Without elaborating, both cops hustled inside, no doubt to grill Russo and Lee about the search warrant.

"Why do I feel like they know more than they're telling?" she asked Mason.

"Because this entire town is suspicious," Mason agreed. "I really hoped that you applying for a teaching job would be a good cover."

"Me too. Especially considering how much they wanted to hire me." She sighed and shook her head. "I hate knowing we're right back where we started, with no idea where to find Lucas."

"I know." Mason wrapped his arm around her shoulders and gave her a quick hug. "But we do know one thing."

"Like what?"

"Sunrise Investments is likely owned and operated by *el jefe*." He stared at the green house. "Getting a list of all their properties and locations is the best way to find Lucas." He snapped his fingers. "Didn't you see two more addresses?"

"Yes." She thought back, then rattled it off.

Mason used his phone to find the location. "The house right next door. Hang on a minute, I'm heading over to check it out."

Aubrey watched as Mason and Bravo headed to the white clapboard house next to the green one. Mason peered through several windows, disappearing around the rear side of the house, before joining her again.

"The place is stripped bare, just like this one." Mason glanced at Bravo. "No alerts on Lucas's scent either."

"I hope he's not in Mexico by now." A cloud of depression weighed on her. She hated knowing she'd let the deaf boy down.

"The thing is they could have taken him to Mexico already," Mason pointed out. "Instead of bringing him here to El Cajon."

"True. Hiding him here makes no sense. Not if he was taken to be used for criminal activities." She couldn't bear to say the words out loud.

"Yeah, that's been bugging me too." Mason noticed her shivering. "Let's wait for Russo and Lee inside the SUV. Looks like this may take a while."

"The local cops didn't look happy," she said once they were settled in the SUV. Mason had taken the driver's seat so that he could hear her better, she knew.

"Could be a turf thing. But they should know if there is criminal activity going on in their backyard."

"Unless they've been paid to look the other way." She sighed. "I'm to the point I don't trust anyone. Except you, Mason."

He reached over to take her hand. "Keep in mind most people can be trusted. It's just that we're dealing with a criminal organization."

She stared at their joined hands for a long moment. "I need to believe we'll find Lucas very soon. I can't bear the thought of failing him."

Mason surprised her by lifting their joined hands to his

lips. He kissed her hand, then released it. "We will. I might head back to Twisted, to check out the rooms above the tavern. Especially knowing the building is owned by Sunset Investments, LLC."

She knew that meant leaving her alone, but what could she say? They'd waited for law enforcement this afternoon, and look how that had turned out. No, she wasn't about to make the same mistake again. "Let's go now," she urged.

"Hold on, there's Russo and Lee." Mason lowered the windows. "Find anything?"

"The place has been wiped clean," Russo said. "Other than Bravo's alerting on the boy's scent, we have no proof the kid was here."

"What do the local police think?" Aubrey asked. "They told me they didn't know who owned the place."

"That's their story," Lee agreed. "They claim nothing suspicious has ever happened here. They don't think much of our judge providing the search warrant."

"I don't care what they think," Russo said. He frowned. "Where are you two headed?"

"Back to the motel," Mason answered before she could say anything. "We need a list of all properties owned by Sunset Investments, LLC."

"I have one of our tech guys pulling that data," Lee informed them. "The house next door is also owned by them, but it looks empty too."

"It is, Mason checked it." Aubrey frowned. "There's at least one other property here."

"We can look, but I doubt they've kept the kid here in El Cajon," Russo said.

Aubrey felt he was probably right about that.

"Will you share the list with us?" Mason asked. "We

can't waste any more time. They've hidden Lucas some-where. Likely closer to the San Diego area."

"Yeah, we'll share it with you," Russo agreed. Lee lifted a brow at that but didn't argue. "Stay safe."

"Will do." Mason lifted the windows and put the rental in gear.

"Are we really heading back to the motel?" she asked.

"Not the one here, but we'll head back to the one we stayed in near East Village." Mason glanced over at her. "I can't bring you and Bravo to Twisted, Aubrey."

"I know." She couldn't blame him. It was obvious Mason worked better alone.

As much as she wanted to be there for Lucas to allay his fears, at this point, she wanted him rescued most of all.

———

MASON WASN'T CONVINCED *el jefe* would take Lucas from El Cajon to the rooms above Twisted, but he couldn't ignore the link to Sunrise Investments.

They made good time heading back to East Village. He drove past Twisted until he found a parking spot a few blocks away.

"Take the SUV and head back to the motel we stayed in earlier," he instructed.

"How will you get back?"

"I'll walk or grab a rideshare." He gave her a stern look. "Do not wait for me, understand? If things go south, I'll need to get far away from the immediate area without worrying about your safety."

"I understand." She looked resigned to her fate. "God be with you, Mason."

"Thanks, and with you too." He slid out from behind

the wheel and waited for her to get into the driver's seat. Then he lightly tapped the hood, indicating she should take off.

He saw her fingers move in a sign language message before she drove away. He stared after her for a moment, wondering if he'd misinterpreted her intent.

Had she signed I love you? Or had he imagined it?

Mason told himself it didn't matter. He needed to get inside the upper level of the building to see if Lucas was there. If not, they could scratch this off their list. No doubt, Russo and Lee would find several other places owned by Sunrise Investments.

Hopefully not so many they couldn't check them out one by one.

Mason went to the fire escape on the building he'd escaped from yesterday. It seemed like hours ago, but at least he was familiar with the area now. He swiftly climbed to the rooftop and then ran and leaped from one building to the next until he'd landed on top of the building that housed Twisted.

The door leading into the building from the roof was locked. He took out a couple of his lock-picking tools and quickly accessed the building. Once he'd stepped inside, he silently closed the door behind him.

Stealth was critical now, and he had to test each stair before putting his weight on it while praying he'd be able to hear if they made noise. The third one down from the top began to creak, so he skipped that one and continued moving. Being in the dark wasn't unusual, the SEALs were often deployed after nightfall, but he missed having his teammates covering his six.

He descended two flights of stairs before he reached a floor containing several closed doors. He inched forward, checking the first one. It wasn't locked. Carrying his weapon in his left hand, he pushed the door open with his right and used a small penlight to quickly scan the room.

Empty.

The next room was unlocked and empty too. In both rooms, the windows had been clearly boarded up. Because they'd used them as jail cells? Or because *el jefe* hadn't bothered to fix the broken or missing windows?

He feared the former rather than the latter.

The third and final door on this floor was locked. He knelt on the floor and used his lock-picking tools to access the room. He didn't want to use his penlight, so it took him longer than usual to get the door open in the dark.

When he felt the lock give, he gently turned the handle. He stayed in a low crouch as he softly pushed the door open. He tried to listen for the sound of a human presence, like breathing or moving around, but he didn't trust his diminished hearing.

He scooted through the door, pressing his back against the wall. The interior of the room was just as dark as the other two had been. It would have been nice to have night vision goggles, but he hadn't anticipated needing a pair as a civilian.

His gut told him the room was empty, but he slid silently across the floor, feeling for anything nearby. He wasn't surprised to find the metal post of a bed. Risking the penlight, he turned it on, holding it above the barrel of his Sig Sauer.

The mattress was bare. Sweeping the light back and forth, he made sure the room was empty before closing the door behind him.

Had Lucas been kept in here at one point? Why was this one locked when the others hadn't been?

Taking his time, he examined the interior of the room more closely. The windows were boarded up, just like the other rooms, although this was the only bed that he'd found.

Not that *el jefe* couldn't have kept Lucas in a room without any furniture at all. He wouldn't put anything past the head of the Blue Devils.

Still, this room reminded him of the bedroom of the green house. Crossing over to the rusted bed frame, he scanned the mattress for signs of recent use. The entire floor smelled musty, the mattress even more so.

The beam of his penlight picked up some scrapes along the side of the wall closest to the head of the bed. Kneeling on the mattress, he peered at the markings more closely.

L-U-C

He blinked, then looked again to make sure he was seeing correctly. The letters weren't neat, or even in a line, but there was no mistaking the fact that the markings had been left intentionally.

Lucas had been there.

Unfortunately, there was no sign of the boy now. Based on the recent sequence of events, Mason had to assume that Lucas had been brought here first, then likely moved to the El Cajon location after he'd shown up yesterday.

Dejected, he turned to leave the way he'd come. But when he opened the door, he felt a vibration through the floor.

Noise from the bar below?

Or someone coming up to investigate?

Mason had no idea if he'd somehow alerted the people below of his presence. Being quiet when you couldn't tell how loud you were was nearly impossible.

He doused the light and swiftly moved down the hallway to the stairs leading up to the roof. He preferred his chances up top where there was more room to maneuver rather than meeting what could be several armed men coming up at him through a very narrow hallway from the bar downstairs.

He'd made it nearly to the top of first flight of stairs when he heard the distinct sound of gunfire. Without pausing, he continued climbing, moving faster now that silence wasn't essential.

Barreling through the door, he moved toward the far edge of the roof. He considered jumping across but changed his mind. He dropped down so that he was sprawled on his stomach, his weapon braced in two hands pointed directly at the roof doorway.

Seconds later, the door burst open, and two armed men came into view. They scanned the area, overlooking him lying on his stomach. He took aim and fired twice, aiming to wound both men rather than to kill them outright.

For two reasons. One, he didn't like killing in general, especially since he wasn't in the middle of a war.

But more importantly to obtain information.

Lucas had been there, likely twenty-four hours ago. Someone in this blasted place had to know something.

The two men yelled in pain as they fell to the ground. He'd purposefully aimed at their thighs, hoping to avoid hitting the very large femoral artery.

Thankfully, these guys were not well-trained soldiers because they both dropped their weapons as they grabbed for their respective wounds.

In a flash, Mason leaped up and ran over, kicking both guns with enough force to send them over the edge of the roof to the ground below.

Maybe the police would find more crimes linked to the guns. He could only hope.

"I'm gonna kill you," one of the men shouted.

Mason leveled his gun at his face. "What's to stop me from finishing you both off here and now?"

The guy blanched, fear widening his eyes.

"I need to find Lucas Espinoza." He closed the door behind them and held it shut with his boot. "Help me and I'll let you live. Refuse and I'll kill you both."

"Why do you care about the dummy?" the second man asked.

Mason pressed the muzzle of his gun against the man's forehead. "Where is he?"

"*El Jefe* has him," the guy whimpered. "We were told to kill anyone asking about the kid."

This wasn't exactly a surprise, except maybe for the order to kill him and anyone else asking about Lucas. "Where is he?"

"He was here, but Jorge took him away late last night," the first man admitted. "Hey, you gotta get me medical help, I'm bleeding bad!"

Mason glanced briefly at his leg wound. "The bullet didn't hit an artery, so you'll be fine. What other businesses does *el jefe* own?"

"Lots," one of them admitted. "Mostly here and in El Cajon."

"I know of the places in El Cajon. What about here in East Village? Or some other suburb of San Diego?"

"I don't know," the whiny man said. "I think he has another couple of bars and a warehouse."

Mason knew he was running out of time. He removed his gun from the man's forehead and hit him on the back of his head. The man fell to the ground.

"You said you wouldn't kill us . . . ," the other protested, but Mason knocked him out too.

He sprinted across the roof and leaped across the opening to the next building. As he was sprinting to the other side, he heard more gunfire.

Reinforcements had arrived.

Thankfully, he'd gotten a pretty good lead. He kept going, praying the men who'd begun shooting at him weren't expert marksmen. He cleared the opening between the second and third buildings and ran hard for the fire escape.

If any of these goofballs had chased him the first time, they'd know his escape route. As he swung over the edge of the building onto the metal fire escape, he glanced down, expecting to see a welcoming committee.

The area below was empty. But he doubted it would be for long.

Mason clamored down the shaky metal staircase as quickly as possible. When he was about six feet from the ground, he let go, dropping to the ground.

He landed awkwardly on his left foot but ignored the flash of pain. He was up and running with every ounce of strength he possessed.

When he was finally safe, he bent at the waist, braced his hands on his thighs, and silently thanked God for protecting him.

CHAPTER THIRTEEN

On the way back to the motel, Aubrey decided to take a detour, swinging past Nanette's apartment building. Maybe if she spoke to Lucas's mother, she could convince the woman to help them find the boy.

The windows of the corner apartment were dark. She parked along the road, staring at them for several moments. Bravo lifted his head to look at her curiously. She stroked his fur, glad to have him beside her. "I honestly don't think she's home."

Bravo thumped his tail in answer.

She pulled away and continued driving, going to the last few places Bravo had alerted on Lucas's scent. The café, the bus stop, then she drove to the restaurant where Nanette worked.

The hostess claimed Nanette wouldn't be in for the rest of the week, but maybe that had changed. It was possible Lucas's mother was working right now. Craning her neck, she watched through the window, but of course, she didn't see Nanette. Or the hostess she'd spoken to, was it only yesterday? She sighed, her heart aching for Lucas.

Keeping the boy hidden in a house in El Cajon really didn't make any sense. The city didn't seem to be a hotbed of human trafficking. Not that she'd toured the entire city, but she had visited the school. The class sizes were small, but the kids had appeared happy and playful rather than withdrawn and sullen.

Why had *el jefe* taken the boy? As a way to control Nanette, Lucas's mother? To make her do something for him? Or for the Blue Devils in general? Is that why Nanette hadn't been in to work her shifts at the restaurant?

If that was the case, why not just take her? If she was gone, Lucas would have ended up in the foster care system. Which had to be less trouble for the Blue Devils than hiding and moving him from one location to the next.

She glanced again at Bravo, feeling as if they were missing something.

There was nothing more she could do here. She drove past the restaurant, turning at the next corner. Her thought was to drive around the block, but she instinctively hit the brakes when a woman wearing the restaurant uniform came running out of the alley, her eyes wide and her hands clamped over her mouth.

The tiny hairs lifted on the back of Aubrey's neck. Without giving herself time to think it through, she threw the gearshift into park, rolled down the window for Bravo, then killed the engine. Grabbing her phone to use as a flashlight, she slid out from behind the wheel and entered the alley.

She'd only taken a few steps when she saw her. Nanette Espinoza, lying on the ground near the restaurant dumpster. Aubrey forced herself to step closer to check for a pulse, but there wasn't one.

Nanette was dead.

And based on the bruising around the woman's neck, she'd been strangled to death.

A wave of dizziness hit hard. There wasn't any blood, but she stumbled away from the body, placing her hand on the brick building to keep herself upright. She quickly dialed 911 but could already hear the wail of sirens growing closer, no doubt notified by the restaurant employee who'd ran from the alley.

When the squad pulled up near the rental, she forced herself to walk over to meet the officers. "I—uh, that's Nanette Espinoza, she's dead. Her ten-year-old son, Lucas, has been missing since Tuesday." Her teeth began to chatter. "I—I need to call Detective Russo."

"Please stay back." One of the officers gently pushed her out of the way. "We'll take over from here."

She ignored him, using her phone to call Detective Russo. Bravo stuck his head through the open window, nudging her cheek. Tears burned her eyes, but she couldn't fall apart. Not yet.

"Russo," he answered curtly.

"It's Aubrey. I—found Nanette—her body. S—she's dead."

"What? Where?"

She swiped at her eyes and sniffled. "In the alley behind the restaurant where she used to work. Next to the dumpster. I—think she's been strangled. Two officers are here."

"Stay put. We're on our way." Russo clicked off.

Her knees threatened to buckle, so she slid into the driver's seat and rested her forehead on the steering wheel.

Nanette was dead. The loss reverberated through her head like a bullet. She'd been strangled. By *el jefe*? Or another of his Blue Devil goons? Why? Was there a reason Lucas's mother had to die?

Was Lucas next?

A headache pounded in her temples. The entire situation weighed heavily on her shoulders. On her conscience.

Lucas couldn't talk, but he could scream for help. And he could probably read lips to a certain extent. He wasn't helpless, but he was vulnerable.

They had to find him. They just had to!

Bravo rested his head in her lap. She wanted to call Mason but didn't dare put him in danger too.

"Ma'am?"

She pulled herself together and looked up at the officer. "Yes?"

"I'll need your statement."

As she explained what had transpired, Russo and Lee arrived. They checked on Nanette's body, then returned to her SUV. Russo told her to start at the beginning, so she went through the story once more.

"Where's Gray?" Russo asked.

She shook her head. "I don't know. We're meeting back at the motel."

Russo glared at her, obviously believing she was holding back. "Which motel?"

"Look, what does that have to do with Nanette?" she demanded. "Don't you understand? Lucas is still missing, and he could be next!"

"I know, I'm sorry." Russo looked exhausted, as did Lee. "We just returned from El Cajon when you called. If you want to go back to the motel, that's fine. We'll follow up with you tomorrow."

"Thanks." Her eyes filled with tears at knowing Lucas was truly an orphan now. As if he wouldn't have enough to deal with once they'd found him. Learning his mother had died could push the boy over the edge.

She left the scene of the murder, feeling sick at heart. When she arrived at the motel, she went inside with Bravo following at her heels. She dropped back onto the bed, fresh tears threatening.

Lifting her gaze to the ceiling, she found herself questioning God's plan. This young deaf boy had already been through so much, was facing so many challenges to learn, why did he have to suffer even more?

There was no answer from above.

Not that she'd expected one. This wasn't her first time asking why. After losing Noah and Carter, Aubrey's conversations with God were of a similar plane. Why her? Why so much loss?

Her phone rang again. Mason! "Are you all right?"

"Yeah, I'm just a couple of blocks away. I wanted to let you know so you don't freak out when I get there."

"Thanks for that." After finding Nanette's body, she would have definitely been alarmed at a knock on the motel room door. "Did you find Lucas?" She couldn't stop herself from asking, even though she knew Mason would have told her immediately if he had.

"No, but I found the room they kept him in, above Twisted. Smart kid scratched the first three letters of his name into the peeling paint on the wall."

She straightened, a sliver of hope lightening her heart. "You think they kept him there before moving him to El Cajon?"

"I do, yes. I'm sure my showing up at Twisted put a wrench in their plan, so that's why they moved him. We'll talk more when I get there, okay?"

"That's fine. See you soon." She lowered her phone, relieved he wasn't hurt. That he'd found the room where

Lucas was kept was encouraging, although it didn't get them any closer to finding him, now.

Five minutes later, Mason tapped on the door. She opened it and couldn't stop herself from stepping into his arms.

"Hey, are you okay?" He sounded concerned as he nudged her farther into the room to allow the door to shut behind them. "Did something happen?"

"Nanette was murdered." She lifted her head so that he'd be able to hear her. "Don't be upset with me, but I drove around before coming back here. I went to the restaurant where she worked and saw one of the employees running out of the alley. I—it looked like she was strangled."

"You found her?" Mason sighed and cradled her close. "That sounds terrible, Aubrey. I'm so sorry."

"Russo and Lee are still there."

"Any suspects?" Mason asked.

"Other than *el jefe* and the entire Blue Devils gang?" She shook her head morosely. "No."

He nodded and continued to hold her. Aubrey could have stayed in his arms forever, but she forced herself to step back.

That's when she noticed the blood. The room spun for a moment, and she reached out to steady herself. "You're hurt!" The words came out as accusatory.

"Just broke the wound open, nothing more." He covered the blood with his hand. "Don't pass out, I'll wash up in the bathroom."

She didn't want to pass out, so she dropped to the edge of the bed, keeping her gaze averted from his reopened injury. "You're not hurt anywhere else?"

"I'm fine." He disappeared into the bathroom.

After taking several deep breaths, she felt better. Her

cheeks flushed with shame. Really, this ridiculous reaction needed to stop. The miscarriage had been ten years ago, she should be over it by now.

In that moment, she thought about Lucas not having a mother. And of how much she wanted a son. She could adopt Lucas or, at the very least, provide a foster home for him. The process of becoming a foster parent wasn't quick, but as a teacher, she had a step up on other potential candidates.

Her background check was already on file with the state, updated every two years as mandated by law. And she knew sign language too. There was always a shortage of good foster homes, many people only signed up to get the monthly stipend. Money she didn't need and would gladly forfeit.

Yes, she could do this. For Lucas, and for herself. The idea filled her with hope, although she wasn't sure how Lucas would feel about it. She wanted to believe he'd be grateful to stay with someone he knew and hopefully liked rather than a stranger. But grief could change a person, especially a young boy.

It had certainly changed her.

For the first time since finding Nanette, Aubrey felt hope for the future.

Maybe this was part of God's plan all along.

MASON WASHED the blood from his arm in the bathroom, reeling at the news of Nanette's murder.

He'd wanted to yell at Aubrey for not going straight back to the motel. She shouldn't have had to stumble over a crime scene. Especially not for a victim she knew.

She was sitting exactly where he'd left her, staring vacantly off into space. He dropped beside her, taking her hand in his. "I'm truly sorry about Nanette."

"Me too." She drew in a deep breath and let it out slowly. "Did you really find Lucas's name scratched in the wall?"

"Yeah. I also spoke to one of the Blue Devils before I had to get out of there. I specifically asked about properties owned by *el jefe*. He acknowledged his boss owned several places here and in El Cajon."

"Did he give any specifics?"

"A couple of taverns and a warehouse here in East Village. I don't suppose Russo or Lee has had time to send over the list of properties owned by Sunrise Investments."

"No, and I honestly didn't think to ask."

Mason grimaced, understanding that finding a dead body would be enough to knock anyone off balance. "We'll follow up tomorrow. For now, we should get some sleep."

"I'll try." She didn't sound enthusiastic.

"Prayer should help, don't you think?" He was a bit surprised at how easy it had been to turn to God. Not just when he needed support but also in gratitude.

He hoped Aubrey would be able to find solace in prayer tonight. The last thing she needed was to have nightmares over what she'd seen.

He took Bravo out for a long walk to give her privacy. Thankfully, she appeared to be asleep by the time he and Bravo returned. Leaving the connecting doorway open, he retreated to his room.

Mason managed to fall asleep, an ability honed through his twenty-two years with the SEALs. The next morning, he woke before Aubrey. Keenly aware of her sleeping in the next room, he silently slid out from the covers, still wearing the clothes he'd had on the day before. He hadn't wanted Aubrey to feel uncomfortable in any way.

Bravo lifted his head, then jumped off the bed to join him. After a quick stop in the bathroom, he took Bravo outside. The day matched his mood—dark and gloomy, the air heavy with the scent of rain.

He hoped it wouldn't storm, possibly impeding the ongoing search for Lucas. The list of properties should help them target the most likely place to find him.

Two taverns and a warehouse would be high on his list. He didn't want to let Russo and Lee know what the guy last night had told him. No more waiting around, wasting time to get a proper search warrant.

This time, he wasn't going to let stupid rules keep him from finding the boy.

He'd deal with the aftermath of breaking the law after Lucas was safe.

His phone buzzed with an incoming call. Kaleb. Mason quickly answered. "What's the news on Ava's disappearance?"

"Nothing good, Nico is still determined to find her. He's trying to track the boyfriend, but there's another lead I'd like to investigate. I wanted to check in with you first, though. I can swing down to San Diego if you still need my help. I can always follow up on my lead later."

Mason hesitated. As much as he wanted Kaleb's help, he felt guilty about Jaydon's death. "Things are under control here, go ahead and follow up on your lead."

"Are you sure?" Kaleb asked. "I don't mind."

"Yeah, I'm sure. You should keep searching for Ava."

"Roger that, Chief." Kaleb disconnected from the call.

He said a silent prayer that Kaleb and Nico would find Ava as he returned to the motel rooms. Aubrey was already showered and dressed. He quickly fed Bravo, realizing he was getting low on food for his K9 partner. "I'll need to stop at a pet supply store today."

"Not a problem." She reached over to stroke Bravo's head. "He's been a great help in tracking Lucas."

And in protecting Aubrey, he silently added. It still irked him that she hadn't come straight to the motel, but there was nothing he could do about that now. "Let's grab something to eat. We can hit the pet supply store on our way back."

She nodded and rose. Moments later, they were at the same family restaurant they'd eaten in yesterday.

"Another day gone," Aubrey said with a sigh. "Lucas was last seen on Tuesday. It's been five days, Mason. I desperately want to believe he's still alive."

"I know." He felt the pressure too. Today was Saturday, they'd been searching for him since Wednesday night.

The fact that Bravo had alerted on the boy's scent as recent as yesterday was encouraging. Bravo wasn't a cadaver dog. And there would be no reason for *el jefe* to move Lucas from El Cajon if he was already dead.

No, he believed *el jefe* wanted Lucas alive for some reason.

"Russo asked me where you were last night," Aubrey said as their meals were served. "I didn't tell him anything, other than we were planning to meet at the motel."

"Thanks." He met her gaze across the table. "I used lock picks to break in to the rooms above Twisted, which means finding Lucas's name on the wall can't be used in a case against *el jefe.*"

"I know." She shrugged. "I hate knowing Lucas is at that man's mercy. I think it's more important to find Lucas, then we can worry about what evidence can be used against his kidnappers."

"We're on the same page, then." He reached over to take her hand. "Once we get that list of properties, I'll search them from top to bottom. I promise, if Lucas is there, I'll find him."

"I believe you." She gripped his hand for a moment. "I wish you'd let me come with you."

He shook his head, gently pulling out of her grasp. "You need to trust in my ability to get this done."

"I do, but sitting around doing nothing isn't easy." She abruptly straightened. "Wait a minute, I can keep searching on the property listings rather than waiting for Russo and Lee. The fact that we're looking specifically for two taverns and a warehouse narrows the field. We can start there."

He nodded slowly. He wasn't as good with searching on the computer, but she'd found the properties belonging to Sunrise Investments in El Cajon, so he was hopeful she'd find the places he'd been told about too. "Okay, after I pick up food for Bravo, we'll go back to the motel. They offer free Wi-Fi for the computer. And I should pay for another night too."

"Good plan." She offered a lopsided smile. "I'm happy to help."

He could relate to her frustration, but the near miss he had last night only strengthened his resolve to keep her out of harm's way.

By the time they'd finished breakfast, dark clouds were continuing to move in. Mason didn't doubt the rain would soon follow. Winter in San Diego usually brought a couple of big rainstorms.

They stopped for dog food, then returned to the connecting rooms at the motel. While Aubrey booted up the computer, he went to the front desk to extend their stay. Thankfully, this wasn't the peak season for tourists, so the clerk gladly gave them the rooms for another night.

He hoped they wouldn't need to stay much longer. Mason wasn't worried about his willpower, he had that in spades thanks to BUD/S training and his years of running ops for the government.

Yet the longer he practically lived with Aubrey, the harder it would be to let her go once this was over.

She was on his mind the first thing in the morning and during his last conscious thoughts at night. In all these years, he'd never thought he'd missed out on anything by staying single. Especially after watching other marriages fail.

But now? He couldn't begin to imagine life without Aubrey.

And that was far scarier than searching a dozen Blue Devils–owned buildings to find Lucas.

He ran through the rain back to their rooms. Aubrey was hunched over the computer, peering intently at the screen.

His skills ran more toward using weapons and taking out tangos rather than computer searches. He sat beside her, idly stroking Bravo's fur. His plan was to use Bravo to locate Lucas's scent at whichever properties Aubrey found, although the rain would make that task problematic.

Bravo might be able to alert on a scent near a covered doorway, but he wouldn't be able to find a scent cone as easily. Especially if the rain was coming down hard.

"I found something," Aubrey said, breaking the silence. "A bar/restaurant called Fourth Base, it's not far from Petco Park."

"I know that place." He frowned. "It's nice, and lots of baseball fans like to go there before and after games."

She lifted a brow. "It's not like Twisted or The Overlook?"

"Not at all." He gestured to the screen. "Pull up their website. I don't think there are apartments or anything above the restaurant."

She did as he asked and shook her head. "Here's what it looks like from the front. Nothing above the restaurant itself, unless it's an attic of some kind."

"Keep searching. I don't think they'd try to hide Lucas in a popular restaurant that does a lot of legitimate business." Although he felt certain the business was used to launder money.

"Okay." She turned back to the computer.

He watched her profile, liking the way she left her hair loose around her shoulders. She looked so different when she donned her schoolteacher persona. Not that she wasn't stunning even wearing her dress slacks and blouses and her hair pulled back from her face, but he preferred her casual look.

And had to curl his fingers into fists to stop from reaching out to touch her hair.

Man, he had it bad. He'd never been so preoccupied with a woman.

He rose and paced the length of the room. Bravo watched him with a knowing look in his dark eyes. As if his partner knew he was on the verge of making a fool of himself.

Not today. Mason told himself to stay focused. Lucas could not end up dead like his mother.

"Okay, I found another bar. This one seems to be more in line with Twisted. Although the name is simply

Hector's." She looked over her shoulder. "Do you know anyone named Hector?"

"No. Do you?"

She shook her head. "I can give you this address too. It does look like there are rooms above the restaurant. But I still haven't found the warehouse."

"Too bad because I could see the warehouse as being a good place to hide a ten-year-old boy." He returned to sit beside her. "You're sure there isn't another place under that name?"

"Not that I've found." She took a small notepad from her bag and wrote down an address. "I think it would be helpful to drive by the place first, especially since it's pouring rain."

He'd run ops in far worse conditions, but he didn't deny the idea had merit. "Okay, let's go."

"The bar doesn't open until ten o'clock." She pulled on her light jacket. "Maybe you can get in and out before there are a bunch of people there."

He nodded in agreement. "Good plan."

They dashed out to the rental. Aubrey jumped into the passenger seat while he took a moment to put Bravo in the back. Soon they were out on the road, heading toward Hector's.

The bar was located several miles in the opposite direction of Twisted. This specific area of East Village held mostly businesses rather than residential homes or apartment buildings.

"Lots of other businesses around," Aubrey observed. "Do you think the bar caters to the people who work nearby?"

"You're assuming Blue Devils actually work," he said dryly.

"If only they'd put as much effort into being productive members of society rather than breaking the law," she agreed.

He drove around the block, looking at the bar from several spots. When he'd done as much as he could from inside the vehicle, he pulled over to the curb. "I'll go on foot from here. Keep Bravo with you, and this time?" He scowled. "Go straight back to the motel."

"Okay, okay." She gestured toward the rain pelting the ground outside. "Call me if you need a ride."

"Once I'm wet, I can't get any wetter." He threw the gearshift into park and slid out of the car. He didn't have high hopes of finding Lucas above Hector's, but maybe it was a place he could cross off their list.

"Lord, give me strength," he whispered, ignoring the rain that soaked him through to the skin in less than five minutes. "Show me the way."

CHAPTER FOURTEEN

Leaving Mason behind was becoming a habit, one she didn't much care for. Aubrey drove slowly down the street away from Hector's, looking for signs on the buildings surrounding the restaurant. There were some without names, but one place was listed as Schroeder's. Repeating the name in her mind, she returned to the motel. Bravo followed her inside, then shook himself, throwing water everywhere.

Aubrey sighed and grabbed a towel from the bathroom to dry off, used another towel for Bravo, then sat behind the computer.

It bothered her that they hadn't found a warehouse belonging to Sunrise Investments, LLC. Especially since the Blue Devil Mason had spoken to had mentioned it. Maybe he'd only said that to lead them astray, but somehow, knowing Mason had gone into every dangerous situation with a gun, and had in fact been forced to use it, she felt certain Mason would put enough fear in the man that he'd tell the truth.

She typed in the name Schroeder, and the property

came up on the screen. It shouldn't have been a surprise that the owner of that warehouse was a man named Joseph Schroeder.

Probably not a member of the Blue Devils, although she knew anything was possible. Just because many of the men who'd they'd come across were Hispanic didn't mean that others weren't involved in the gang.

Greed knew no boundaries.

She stared at the screen, then narrowed her gaze on the address. Using the same motel notepad as before, she wrote down the address of both Hector's restaurant and of Schroeder's warehouse.

It was a tedious process to search for similar addresses. She found one owned by a man named Benito Gonzales. She frowned, rolling the name through her mind. It seemed familiar, but she couldn't put her finger on where she'd heard it before.

She continued searching on addresses when it hit her. The name Benito Gonzales had been on another property. Switching her search function, she typed in the name and sucked in a harsh breath.

There was a house in El Cajon that was also owned by Benito Gonzales.

El jefe? Her heart pounded in her chest. Maybe, although she couldn't know for sure. Gonzales could very well be another guy who happened to own two properties, one in East Village and one in El Cajon.

No, even she couldn't make herself believe it. The location of the warehouse being close to Hector's was too much of a coincidence. That, and knowing other properties in El Cajon had been used by the Blue Devils, was a link that was impossible to ignore.

Grabbing her phone, she quickly dialed Russo. The call

went to his voice mail, so she told him what she'd found with instructions to call her back. She wanted to call Mason, too, but hesitated. What if he was in a dangerous position? Even with the phone on silent, the screen would light up at her call, alerting anyone nearby of his location.

She looked at Bravo. "We have to warn Mason. He could be in danger."

Bravo cocked his head, his dark eyes seeming to agree with her assessment.

The rain was still pouring down in buckets. Not that she was going to let the inclement weather hold her back. Especially if Mason's life was in danger.

She put her phone on silent, tucked it into the inside pocket of her jacket to keep it protected from the rain as much as possible, then shrugged into the still soaked garment. Mason was right, once you were wet, you couldn't get any wetter.

But as she headed outside, the cool wind made her shiver. She may not get any wetter, but she sure could get colder.

Get over it, she told herself sternly. *Think of Mason and Lucas.*

She brought Bravo along for the ride, why, she wasn't sure. Maybe because she didn't want to go alone, although she didn't dare put the dog in danger either. Driving through the deluge, she returned to the area where Hector's was located.

It was still early enough that the restaurant wasn't open. Staff could be arriving any time, though, to set up. The warehouse owned by Benito Gonzales was very close to Hector's. The place appeared deserted, but she knew based on the green house they'd found in El Cajon that looks could be deceiving.

She drove past until she found a place to park the rental SUV. The spot was near Schroeder's, which she hoped wasn't a mistake. It wouldn't be good if Schroeder's was actually the warehouse where Lucas was being held. Yet she didn't think it was.

Bravo sat tall in the seat beside her. She looked at him.

"I'm going to leave the windows open a bit for you, okay?" Oddly, she found comfort in talking to the dog. "I know the rain will get inside, but I think that's better for you in the long run. Especially if something happens and we can't get back here to take care of you."

The thought made her stomach clench. Should she take Bravo back to the motel? Indecision clawed at her. Finally, she lowered the windows and pushed open her driver's side door, stepping out into the rain. This wouldn't take long. All she needed to do was warn Mason.

And if she couldn't find him, she'd take a quick peek inside the warehouse. It could very well be sitting empty, making this nothing more than a wild-goose chase.

Fifteen minutes tops and she'd be back.

Right? Right.

Hunching her shoulders, she dashed through the rain. It was still coming down hard, which wasn't helpful. Still, these storms were known to blow in and out in a matter of hours.

This one would end soon, she hoped.

In trying to think like Mason, she approached Hector's from the rear of the building rather than the front. She tried the back door, but it was locked.

Rain seeped down the back of her neck, soaking her to the skin. Shivering in the cold, she glanced over toward the warehouse. Her eyes widened in shock when she noted a side door hanging ajar.

Was Mason inside already? She didn't hesitate but hurried over to the building, creeping up to the doorway as silently as possible.

That's when it occurred to her that Mason may not be able to hear her or anyone else approaching over the sound of the pelting rain. Hovering in the doorway, she could hear the rain was loud on the metal roof of the warehouse. She edged inside, pausing for a moment to give her eyes time to adjust to the lack of light.

The warehouse wasn't empty, there were boxes stacked nearby, but the building was also divided into rooms. In the distance, she could see the faint glow of a small light.

Instinctively, she knew Mason wasn't the one holding the light. Again, she was torn by indecision. Should she go in farther?

Or turn around and go back to Bravo? She could call Russo again, but if he didn't answer, she wouldn't be any farther ahead. And if Russo didn't answer but called her, the phone would alert others she was hiding there.

She wasn't cut out for this kind of thing, but she couldn't leave. Not yet. Not until she knew who was in the warehouse.

Slipping past the highly stacked boxes, she made her way closer to the light. Was there living space back there? Puddles of water on the floor indicated someone had recently come before her. Glancing back, the water sluicing off her was adding to those same puddles.

The water could have been left by anyone who'd come inside from the pouring rain. She hoped that person was Mason. A hand reached out and grabbed her arm. She nearly cried out, but another hand clamped over her mouth.

Fear spiked but then receded when she heard Mason's whisper. "Why are you here?"

He released her, but in the dim light, she could see his deep scowl. Rather than risking talking, she used sign language. *This warehouse is owned by Benito Gonzales, he also owns a house in El Cajon. He could be el jefe.*

Mason gave a curt nod of understanding. Then he signed back, *Get out while I keep looking around.*

She reluctantly nodded, knowing she was only a liability to him. She took a cautious step back, then froze when she heard a grunting sound. She tried to grasp Mason's arm, but he'd already moved away and out of reach.

The sound was similar to that made by deaf people, especially those who were born that way. Their screams and cries were guttural compared to that of hearing people. Mainly because they could push the cry out of their throat but had no idea what it sounded like.

Lucas? Hope filled her heart. Was the child still alive and being held somewhere inside the warehouse?

She moved closer to the opening between the rooms. The light was a small glow in the sea of darkness. And if not for the pounding rain hitting the metal roof with enough force to sound like golf-sized hail balls, she may have been able to hear talking.

There had to be a reason Lucas had made that sound. It hadn't been her imagination.

Her cochlear implant had changed her life, but it was located only in her right ear. Still, she could hear through it at 100 percent, which was better than what Mason was dealing with.

Had he heard the sound Lucas made? Would he know what it was even if he had? Not knowing the answers to those questions was enough to convince her to stay right where she was.

She crouched down beside the opening between the

rooms and took her phone from the inside pocket of her jacket. It was only slightly damp to the touch. She edged farther away from the doorway, holding the phone close to her chest to minimize the light from the screen.

Time to call the police since she felt certain that grunting sound had come from Lucas. She noted a missed call from Russo along with a voice mail message. The phone's internal dictation allowed her to read his response.

We'll run a search on Benito Gonzales but stay where you are so I can let you know what we find out.

Yeah, too late for that, she thought. Rather than calling 911, she sent him a quick text message. *I'm with Mason. We're in the warehouse owned by Gonzales, and I think Lucas is here too.*

Get out, was Russo's curt response.

She was tempted to do as he asked, but she heard the grunting sound again, almost as if the boy was crying out in pain.

The tiny hairs lifted on the back of her neck. What in the world was going on? Where was Mason? Was he close enough to the light to see the boy?

She told herself to move forward, to do whatever was necessary to save Lucas. Shutting her phone off, she slipped it back into her pocket and eased forward to peer through the opening.

All she could see was more boxes. The room with the light must be in the next room. As she made her move through the opening, something wet and furry brushed against her.

She nearly screamed but then realized the newcomer was Bravo. How had the dog gotten out of the SUV? She didn't think she'd left the windows open far enough for him to get out, but she must have. She winced. Mason would not be happy if something bad happened to Bravo, and it would be all her fault.

Too late now.

She moved silently into the next room, taking refuge behind a stack of boxes. She didn't see Mason, but as Bravo disappeared from sight, she knew the dog would find his owner without difficulty.

Mason would be mad at her, and she couldn't blame him. Yet all she could do was continue praying that God would keep them all safe.

Mason, Lucas, and Bravo too.

———

MASON WASN'T happy that Aubrey had shown up inside the warehouse. His orders for her to stay at the motel had been very clear. A Senior Chief's orders were always followed by his men. Figured, Aubrey didn't listen. Granted, the information she'd provided related to Benito Gonzales owning this warehouse and a home in El Cajon was interesting. It was highly likely that Benito and *el jefe* were one and the same.

Now, they just needed to find a way to prove it.

After spending several minutes looking through Hector's, he'd found nothing remotely interesting. It looked like a legitimate business, although the location here near the warehouses left a lot to be desired. That alone was suspicious. As he'd left the restaurant, locking the door behind him so no one would know he'd been there, he'd noticed the side door of the warehouse had been wetter than it should have been if it had been closed the entire time because of a small overhang up above. Almost as if the door had gotten wet because someone had gone inside.

Curious, he'd decided to head over to investigate.

He'd stumbled across two guards, one just inside the doorway. The guy tried to hit him, but Mason had easily taken him down, then pressed on his carotid arteries to make him pass out. He'd dragged him over to the side, out of the way. Finding duct tape, he bound the man's wrists and ankles, then put tape over his mouth too. The second one had emerged shortly afterward, but he'd taken him out, too, securing him the same way. Both men were alive but down for the count.

How many more? He wasn't sure. And it was more concerning that he hadn't heard Aubrey. It was impossible for him to hear anything over the rain hitting the roof above, but he had thankfully caught a glimpse of her moving toward the doorway. Just in time for him to stop her.

He cautiously made his way toward the lighted area of the warehouse, sweeping his gaze over the area in case there were more guards. The puddles he left in his wake were like a neon sign announcing his path through the building, but there wasn't anything he could do about it. The only good news was that he was so wet that each step left pockets of water behind rather than actual boot prints.

He took another step toward the dim light. He needed to get a visual, to see if Lucas was being held in there or not. He hoped the kid was just tied up and there weren't any Blue Devils standing guard over him. But experience told him to expect the worst.

The only easy day was yesterday. The Navy SEAL mantra echoed in his head.

He eased forward another step. The smell of wet dog made him freeze. A second later, Bravo was at his side, nosing his hand. He put a warning hand on the dog's head, irritated all over again that Aubrey had brought Bravo along. And why hadn't she left the dog in the SUV in the first place? That way she and Bravo would already be on their way back to the relative safety of the motel.

He gave Bravo the hand signal for go, but the animal didn't move. Because the dog couldn't see very well in the darkness? Or because he was alert to the danger? Mason swallowed his anger and continued edging toward the rear portion of the warehouse. He paused again when he heard a strange noise.

What was that? Had he really heard something?

Or had he imagined it?

He had no way of knowing. Even his attempts to move silently were difficult to judge since he couldn't hear what, if any, noise he was making. All he could do was move the way he'd been trained to sneak through forests, deserts, and other rough terrain.

Although it did make him think he should consider getting one of those cochlear implants that Aubrey had touted. This not hearing well thing was getting tiresome.

And dangerous.

Paired as a team, he and Bravo carefully approached the next room. As he grew closer, Mason could see the light shining a bit brighter now. Holding his Sig Sauer in one hand, he gave Bravo the hand signal for sit with the other. Thankfully, his K9 partner complied.

Mason peeked around the corner, then ducked as a shot rang out, chipping the wood near the location where his head had been.

"Throw down your weapon," a voice called out, "or I'll kill the kid."

Mason inwardly winced, wondering how he'd been discovered. Hidden cameras? He hadn't seen any. Maybe he'd made noise during his approach. He hoped and prayed his lack of hearing didn't result in Lucas being killed.

Please, Lord, save Lucas!

The silent prayer gave him a sense of calm, much like he'd experienced when going into hostile and dangerous situations. Was it possible God had always been there for him, even back then? Mason believed He was.

For now, he focused on the present. "How can I trust you not to hurt the boy?" he called, slowly straightening.

A harsh laugh echoed from the room. "You can't trust me, as you should know by now."

The voice wasn't familiar. So likely not one of the men from the Blue Devils he'd interacted with over the past two days.

El jefe himself? Maybe. His quick glance hadn't caught much other than the area was set up as living space. He'd only caught a glimpse of one man and a boy. If the man was *el jefe*, he was surprised there were only two guards.

Unless he'd somehow taken the guy by surprise by showing up at all. For all he knew, there could be dozens of Blue Devils on the way there, ready to pounce as they wasted time chitchatting.

Not a comforting thought.

"Let the kid go and no one has to get hurt," Mason said loudly. "I don't care what the *Diablos Azules* criminal enterprise entails, I'm only here for the boy."

A flash of movement caught the corner of his eye. He swallowed a curse when he realized Aubrey hadn't left the warehouse.

He drilled her with a narrow look and jerked his head toward the doorway they'd come through. She used sign language to explain why she was still here. *I heard Lucas, he's being held close by. Are you hurt?*

Maybe that was the noise he'd heard, but she wasn't telling him something he didn't already know. He signed in response. *Fine, go back, get help.*

Russo is on his way.

"Come out now!" the voice barked.

A grunting, keening noise followed, and Mason understood Lucas was crying out in pain.

"Okay, I'm coming." Mason lifted his hands up so that his Sig Sauer was pointed at the ceiling. "Don't hurt Lucas, he's no risk to you."

"So you think," the voice replied with a sneer. "Drop the gun and kick it away."

Mason couldn't see the face of the man talking. It appeared the man was sitting in a chair, holding Lucas in front of him. The boy's eyes were wide with terror, his cheeks damp with tears. Mason felt bad for the boy, but he was equally thankful he was alive.

At least, for now.

Taking his sweet time, Mason slowly bent and dropped his Sig Sauer on the floor. Then he used his foot to kick it away, toward the left side of the room. If things went south, Aubrey might be able to get her hands on it. He straightened and lifted his hands in the air, palms facing forward. He kept his gaze on the dark shadow behind Lucas. "Okay, I'm not armed. Now what?"

"Step closer," the man invited.

Mason did so, still trying to distinguish the man's facial features mostly hidden behind Lucas's head. He wanted very badly to use sign language to reassure the boy but didn't dare move his hands. He didn't trust Mr. Happy-Trigger-Finger not to shoot.

Then he noticed the boy's gaze track to Mason's left. Imperceptibly, the boy relaxed and didn't look nearly as afraid. Mason hid a smile, realizing Aubrey must have used sign language to reassure the boy.

"You have caused me a lot of manpower," the stranger continued. "Injured and dead men, and for what? Nothing!"

Lucas continued glancing over to Mason's left. The way the man had him positioned in front of him, basically using the kid as a human shield, meant that he didn't know where Lucas was looking. Which was a good thing or the idiot would likely shoot in that direction, just to make a point.

Despite his early annoyance with Aubrey, he was glad to have her hiding in the shadows now. Anything to help put the boy at ease even for a few minutes.

Mason still had his MK 3 knife, but he needed a way to get Lucas away from the man holding him. "I wouldn't consider Lucas nothing," he countered wryly.

"He's useless to me," the man snarled. "His mother lied!. He's completely useless!" The way his voice rose in anger worried Mason. The guy was on the edge of losing control.

"Tell me, Benito Gonzales, do you plan to kill both of us?"

The man jerked involuntarily, making Lucas wince.

"You are also known as *el jefe*, I believe," Mason went on, stalling for time. Russo had to get here sooner or later.

Preferably sooner.

The man he believed to be Gonzales said nothing in response.

"I will say your men have a keen sense of loyalty to you," Mason went on. "They only talked when I threatened to kill them." He forced a smile. "Much like you're doing with a ten-year-old boy."

"Enough!" the man thundered. "You're finished!"

Mason tensed, expecting to be shot dead at point-blank. He didn't have any regrets, other than not telling Aubrey how much he loved her.

He gave Bravo the signal for attack. At the same moment, Lucas went limp, sagging away from the man holding him. Bravo darted forward, barking like crazy, catching Gonzales off guard. Mason quickly drew his knife and threw it at the man sitting in the chair, hitting him to the right of center of his chest.

A look of surprise widened Gonzales's eyes as he aimed the gun at him and pulled the trigger. Mason ducked and rolled, going closer to the guy's chair as Bravo grabbed the man's ankle with his mouth and bit down, hard.

Gonzales howled in pain. Lucas broke free of his grip and made a run for it. Mason didn't take his eyes off Gonzales as the boy ran away, heading straight toward the corner where Aubrey was waiting.

He reached up to grab Gonzales by the neck with his right hand while snagging the weapon from his grip with his left hand. Despite all his tough talk, disarming the guy was easy.

Thanks to Bravo.

"Police!" The shout from the doorway was more than welcome. "Throw down your weapons and come out with your hands up!"

"There are two unconscious men tied with duct tape in the warehouse and this man here who is no longer armed," Mason called out.

"We have the other two Blue Devils," the same voice said.

"Mason, are you okay?" Aubrey's voice was shaky. "I have Lucas, he seems fine."

He didn't immediately answer because up close he

finally recognized the man who'd held Lucas hostage. Who'd used the boy as a human shield and would have very likely killed him if necessary.

The same man who'd been in the picture on Nanette Espinoza's nightstand.

Lucas's father.

"Why?" Mason asked, truly confused. "Why did you take him?"

Gonzales was moaning and crying, his hand near the knife embedded in his chest. Before Mason could warn him not to do it, the idiot pulled the knife out.

Blood squirted from his chest wound. Mason ducked his head to avoid getting doused in the face. He shucked off his jacket and pressed it against the wound, but he knew it wouldn't be enough to stanch the artery the tip of his knife had pierced.

Gonzales continued to moan, but the sound was weak. Mason could see the man's face turning pale as he continued to bleed out.

"Why?" he repeated, shaking the man in frustration. "Why did you do it?"

But it was too late. Benito Gonzales was dead.

CHAPTER FIFTEEN

Aubrey took Lucas outside and crawled into the back of Russo's car with the boy. She could see Mason standing with Bravo beside him, talking at length to Lee about how events had unraveled.

Lucas gripped her tightly, his face buried against her chest. She wanted nothing more than to comfort him, and she would gladly spend the rest of her life doing so if given the chance, but right now, the police needed to know what happened to him over these past few days. And what he may have witnessed.

She silently prayed for his emotional well-being.

With one hand, she gently lifted his face so she could look into his eyes. His dark gaze clung to hers, then filled with tears. She cradled him close again, shaking her head at Russo who was watching through the rearview mirror. "I don't think he's going to be able to tell us anything."

"Okay, then we should have him taken to the closest children's hospital to be examined." Russo already had the car running, heat blaring from the vents. "We need to know if he was hurt—physically."

She closed her eyes for a moment, knowing exactly what he meant. Then she reluctantly nodded. "I need to explain that to him, or he won't understand."

The rear passenger door opened, and Mason slid in beside them with Bravo crowding them even farther. "Friend, Bravo," Mason said, putting his hand on the boy. "Lucas is a friend."

Lucas lifted his head and looked at the dog. It was a little surprising that there wasn't any fear in the boy's eyes. She gently patted Lucas's arm so that he would look at her. With one hand, she signed as she spoke out loud, "*This is my friend, Mason. He helped save us tonight. And that's Bravo, he helped too.*"

Lucas glanced at Mason and nodded. He signed, *I like Bravo. He and Mason are good guys, right?*

She nodded. *Yes, they are. Please, I need to know if you're hurt.*

Bravo is brave, Lucas signed, his mind obviously preoccupied by the dog.

Yes. Are you hurt? she repeated.

He shook his head, but she wasn't sure she could believe him.

Easing farther away, she quickly used both hands to explain, again speaking out loud for Russo's benefit. And also as a way to help Lucas learn to lip-read. It was a common tactic she used every day in the classroom. "*We need a doctor to examine you, okay? To make sure no one hurt you.*"

He shook his head again, then signed back, *I'm not hurt but my mamma* . . . Tears spilled down his cheeks. *He killed her.*

"*I know, I'm so sorry.*" Aubrey couldn't prevent her own eyes from welling up. No child should have to witness his mother's murder. She exchanged a knowing glance with Mason. He nodded at her reassuringly. She knew this was important, so she continued. *"Who was the man who hurt your mother?"*

El Jefe.

Mason tapped Lucas's shoulder so the boy would look at him. He signed as he asked, *"Who is el jefe? The man who had you in the warehouse? Or someone else?"*

Man in warehouse. There was a pause before Lucas added, *He is the devil.*

"He claims the man is the devil, which could mean the Blue Devils," she said out loud to Russo. "Or just an evil man who killed his mother."

"He saw that?" Russo asked, his expression grim. "How awful."

"Yes, it is. He'll need counseling for sure." Aubrey turned her attention back to Lucas. The boy had his hand on Bravo's head, and the dog remained still, seeming to understand how much the child needed him. Again she spoke and signed at the same time. *"Did you stay with the devil the whole time you were gone from school?"*

Lucas shook his head, no. *First, Jose took me to be with another man, one with a scar here.* Lucas touched his cheek. She remembered the mug shot of Raymond Nassar who had a deep scar in his cheek. *Then they gave me something that made me sleepy. When I woke up, the devil and my mom were there. They had a huge fight. I saw them yelling at each other but couldn't understand everything they said.*

Aubrey glanced again at Mason, wondering if the fight had been over Lucas's deafness or the fact that Nanette had taken the boy from his father. Russo frowned in the front seat. "What did he say?"

She explained what Lucas saw, then focused again on the boy. *"Then what happened?"*

Lucas's lower lip trembled. *The devil killed her, then brought me here.*

Mason took over the questioning, drawing Lucas's gaze. Mimicking her lead, he also spoke out loud as he signed. *"Do you know why the devil wanted you? Do you know why he told Jose to take you away from your mom?"*

Lucas didn't answer for a long moment. Finally, he began to sign. *The devil said I belonged to him. That my mamma had no right to take me away. But that I was useless to him now. I would never be able to help run his empire because I can't hear or speak.*

Aubrey blew out a heavy sigh. She repeated what Lucas said for Russo's sake, then added, "I can only think that Nanette took Lucas away when he was young to protect him, but somehow Gonzales found out. He arranged to get his son back, but it wasn't until the big fight that he learned the boy was deaf and unable to speak."

"Which would explain why he called him nothing, then used him as a way to get to me," Mason added. "He wanted revenge for the way I'd injured so many of his men. Although I'm not sure how he knew I was in the warehouse."

"He must have heard you approaching, or maybe one of the guards warned him that an intruder was there." Aubrey shook her head helplessly. "It's unbelievable to think that Gonzales didn't know his own son was deaf."

"Could be that was the reason she took off," Mason pointed out. "I recognized Gonzales from the photograph hidden behind one of Lucas I found on Nanette's bedside table. Lucas was a baby in that picture."

"I guess we'll never know if Nanette was part of the Blue Devils or not," she said with a sigh.

"I can shed some light on that," Russo said. "Nanette Espinoza wasn't her real name; her ID and social security numbers were fake. Her real name is Margarita Juarez. Her, ah, prints popped in the system because she was arrested several years ago for prostitution."

So the skateboarder was right. Aubrey was hit by a wave of regret. If only she'd known. She could have done so much more for Nanette. Then she frowned, her stomach clenching with fear. "Wait a minute, what about Lucas?"

"He was born here in the US," Russo said quickly. "No need to worry about that. I'll notify Child Protective Services that we found him."

"I would like Lucas to stay with me, if possible." She darted a glance at Mason. "He's better off with someone who can communicate with him."

"Of course, he should stay with us," Mason said. "But we'll need to go through formal channels. With Russo's help, I'm sure we can convince CPS to place Lucas with us temporarily, on an emergency basis, until we can go through the formal paperwork."

"With us?" She stared at him. Why was he including himself in this? "I—don't understand."

Lucas was looking between the two of them, clearly trying to grasp the conversation. Feeling guilty, she quickly signed as she spoke. "*Lucas, would you be willing to stay with me for a while? After we get you checked out at the hospital,*" she added, knowing there was no way around that.

"*I'm going with you to the hospital,*" Mason said and signed.

Bravo too? Lucas asked.

"Yes, Bravo too. We're a team." Mason looked at her. *"A really great team."*

Aubrey wasn't sure what to say to that. She was afraid that Mason was just trying to smooth things over for Lucas, especially since the young boy had already formed an attachment to Bravo.

But once their lives went back to normal, she was pretty sure Mason would fade out of her life. The very idea filled her with sorrow, but she could certainly understand. Mason had no idea what it was like to be tied down to a family. She wasn't naïve enough to believe everything with Lucas would go smoothly. Just the opposite.

The boy would forever be emotionally scarred by what he'd suffered the past few days. He may get angry, lash out, get into trouble.

This wouldn't be an easy road. But one she intended to travel with Lucas, no matter what.

Deep down, she knew this was God's plan. Despite the terrible things Lucas had seen, she believed that she had the ability to help the boy survive and thrive.

To succeed.

Glancing again at Mason, she flushed when she realized he was watching her closely. It occurred to her she hadn't thanked him for saving their lives.

"Thank you, Mason. For everything. Without you, Lucas and I wouldn't be sitting here."

"Oh, I think you did your fair share." Mason arched his brow. "I asked you to leave the warehouse, but you didn't. I wasn't too happy about that. Good thing there weren't other Blue Devils hiding in there to hurt you."

She winced. "I didn't know about them at the time, but I couldn't have left. Not when I knew Lucas was there."

"I know." Mason smiled down at the boy curled against

her. Lucas was resting with his eyes closed yet keeping one hand on Bravo's head. "It was good you could reassure him. And you helped him get away."

She smiled wryly. "You may be right about how we make a good team."

"We do." Mason looked as if he wanted to say more, but Russo pulled up to the emergency department of the children's hospital in San Diego.

"Let's get Lucas inside," the detective said.

Aubrey nodded. She felt certain Mason would offer his support in the upcoming days, which was sweet.

But he had his own life to live, one that didn't include a ready-made family.

A clean break may be better for all of them in the long run.

AFTER AUBREY HELPED Lucas get out of the car, he and Bravo quickly joined them. The rain had finally stopped, but they were all soaked to the skin, and he noticed Aubrey was shivering.

His attempt to subtly include himself in her plans hadn't worked. Mason couldn't be sure if that was simply because Aubrey didn't feel the same way toward him as he did or if she was too focused on Lucas.

Either way, he wasn't about to give up.

SEALs never gave up. *Never.*

The staff quickly escorted Lucas to a room. The nurse frowned as he and Bravo crowded in next to Aubrey and Russo. "No dogs allowed."

"He's a service animal." Okay, technically not, but

Lucas made a grunting noise and reached toward the dog. "See? Bravo will help keep Lucas calm."

"Lucas is also deaf and unable to speak," Aubrey added.

The nurse gave up the fight. "Okay, fine. But you need to know that if that dog bites someone, we will press charges."

"He won't unless I give him the command." Mason smiled. "And I would only do that for bad guys."

The nurse smiled, thinking he was joking. He wasn't.

The doctor examined Lucas and deemed him somewhat malnourished but otherwise fine. They took blood for testing, which may show some remnants of the drugs he'd been given. Before they could leave, though, the social worker came in. Mason smiled as Aubrey laid out her case for taking Lucas in on an emergency basis.

"I need to talk this over with CPS," the woman said. She glanced at Lucas and said loudly as if he were hard of hearing rather than completely deaf, "Lucas, do you want to stay with Ms. Clark?"

Lucas turned to look at Aubrey who signed and said, *"She wants to know if you are willing to stay with me for a few days."*

Yes. Lucas nodded in emphasis.

"I'll be right back." The social worker disappeared.

"Does that happen often?" Mason asked, signing for Lucas's benefit. *"People talking loudly as if that will help the deaf hear them?"*

"Yes." Aubrey shrugged and turned to include Lucas in the conversation. *"It would help more if they would just speak slower so that deaf people could read their lips easier, right, Lucas?"*

The boy nodded. *I'm hungry.*

"*We'll get you something to eat when we're able to leave,*" Aubrey promised.

The social worker asked Aubrey to come talk to the CPS caseworker. Lucas looked up at the two men warily, then settled his gaze on Mason. *I don't want to live with strangers.*

"*Aubrey will do everything she can to make sure you're able to stay with her.*" Mason paused, then added, "*And Bravo and I will stick around too, just to make sure you're both safe.*"

Good. Lucas looked relieved. *I don't want more bad devils to come after me.*

"*They won't,*" Mason assured him. "*I won't let them. And neither will Bravo.*"

Lucas nodded. He reached out for Bravo, who had stayed right next to his bed. A few minutes later, Aubrey returned. She smiled at Lucas. "*I have permission to take you to my home for the next few weeks. Are you ready to go?*"

Yes, with Mason and Bravo too. Lucas sat up and swung his legs over the edge of the bed.

Aubrey shot him a quick glance but didn't argue. Russo stepped forward. "I'll need to talk to Lucas again, and to both of you, too, but that can wait until tomorrow."

"Thanks." Mason shook the detective's hand. "Appreciate that."

Russo shook his head. "I'm the one who should be thanking you. We wouldn't have cracked this case without your help, Gray." The cop looked at Lucas. "Take good care of that kid."

"That's the plan." Mason hesitated, then asked, "I almost forgot, we left the SUV somewhere near the warehouse."

"At Schroeder's," Aubrey added.

"I'll drop you off there," Russo agreed.

After they picked up their rental, with Lucas and Bravo tucked in the back seat like bosom buddies, Mason drove to the closest fast-food restaurant. Once they had their meals, Mason drove to Aubrey's home.

He felt Aubrey's curious gaze on him but did his best to ignore it. He brought in the bag of dog food he'd purchased what felt like hours earlier, carrying it into the kitchen.

"You don't really have to stay," Aubrey said as Lucas sat down to eat.

"I promised Lucas I would." He turned to face her. "But that's not the real reason I'm staying."

"It's not?"

"No." Mason took a step closer, capturing her hand in his. "I want to be here, Aubrey. For you and for Lucas. And also for me."

She opened her mouth to ask a question, closed it, then frowned. "I'm not sure I understand."

"*I've fallen in love with you.*" He spoke the words and signed them at the same time. "*I understand you may need time, but I want you to know I'm in this for the long haul.*"

Aubrey blushed, darted a glance at Lucas who was watching them intently, and then back at him. "*This won't be easy,*" she warned. "*I promised to take Lucas to family counseling.*"

"*The only easy day was yesterday, remember?*" He smiled and nodded. "*Glad to hear about the counseling. I'll come with you. And you should know by now, SEALs are tough.*" He took another step closer and drew her into his arms. He stopped signing now, whispering, "You should know I don't scare easily."

"Oh, Mason. Are you sure about this? It's a lot to ask . . ."

His answer was to kiss her.

Thankfully, she didn't resist but melted against him, returning his embrace. He would have held her in his arms for the rest of the day and throughout the night except Lucas clapped and laughed.

Mason reluctantly lifted his head and glanced at Lucas. "I can see he's going to be a handful."

Aubrey chuckled. "Oh, you have no idea. And there's still plenty of time for you to back out if it turns out to be too much."

He sighed. "SEALs don't back down."

She stared up at him. "Mason, you are the strongest, sweetest, most exasperating man I've ever met. And you should know I've fallen in love with you too. But this is a really big commitment . . ."

"Say that again," he interrupted.

"Say, what?"

He touched her cheek. "That you love me."

She lifted her hands and signed, *I love you.*

He grinned, swept her into his arms, and swung her around the small kitchen. Bravo looked up at them, then lowered his head. Mason felt certain the dog already understood this was his new family.

Animals were often smarter than people.

"Silly man," Aubrey chided. "Put me down. Our food is getting cold."

"As if I care about that," he teased, but he set her on her feet. He kissed her again, then drew her to the table. Looking directly at Lucas, he signed, *"I love Aubrey with my whole heart. Someday soon, I'm going to convince her to marry me."*

"Marry you?" Aubrey echoed.

"Yeah. But don't worry, I'll ask you properly when you're ready."

"Ready?" She echoed again. The expression on her face would have been comical if not for the uncertain look in Lucas's eyes as he tried to understand his role in all of this. Mason realized the boy felt left out, which hadn't been his intention at all.

Aubrey instantly understood and reached out to touch Lucas's hand. *"You will always have a home with us. I know you miss your mom, but I hope you will become a part of our family."* She touched Mason's arm and Bravo too. Then she signed, *"I love you,"* as she rested her hand over Lucas's heart.

The boy didn't look convinced.

Mason nodded and leaned forward. *"We have been searching for you since Wednesday, and we weren't going to stop until we'd found you."*

Lucas's dark eyes filled with tears and suddenly he threw himself into Aubrey's arms, his slender shoulders shaking with guttural sobs. Mason knew Aubrey was right about this being a long process, but he didn't mind. In fact, he was even more determined to make it work.

Mason wrapped his arms around both Aubrey and Lucas, a knot of emotion lodged in his throat.

After twenty-two years as a single guy, trying to find his place in the civilian world, he'd finally found it. Thanks to God's grace and guidance, he'd found exactly what he didn't even know he was looking for.

His family.

EPILOGUE

Three weeks later . . .

Aubrey finished the dishes, feeling nervous as she dried her hands on a towel. Today the social worker from CPS would come for her final visit. Because of Lucas's special need for sign language, she'd already been approved as his temporary foster parent.

The outcome of today's meeting would decide the future.

She'd made her intent of adopting Lucas clear from the beginning. As expected, Lucas experienced good days and bad days. The twice-weekly counseling had helped, and to her surprise, Mason was a stabilizing force in those sessions.

Sometimes she wondered how he could be so—*patient.*

"Don't worry, everything is going to be fine." Mason had adopted her practice of speaking and signing at the same time. It was so instinctive now that they both did it even when Lucas wasn't around.

She can't make me leave. Lucas's expression was stubborn. He'd gained some weight over the past three weeks and had gotten better at sign language and lipreading.

Best of all, he seemed happy with them.

It was a little odd to have Mason staying with them at her small house. Every time she'd tried to convince him to go back home, he'd resisted. And if she were honest, she'd admit having his help had gotten her and Lucas through this.

And if she had to force herself to let him go after they'd kissed good night, she figured that was her problem.

"Behave and you won't have to go anywhere," Mason pointed out.

Lucas scowled. The doorbell rang, so she hurried over to answer it.

"Ms. Chapman, please come in." Aubrey greeted the social worker. The department of Child Protective Services had found a social worker fluent in sign language, which was a blessing.

"Hello, Aubrey." Ms. Chapman turned to Lucas. *"How are things going for you?"*

Great. I like it here, and I don't want to leave. Lucas wasted no time in getting straight to the point.

"I'm glad to hear that." Ms. Chapman glanced at Mason, then at Aubrey. *"The family counselor has been very impressed with Lucas's progress."*

"You mean with our *progress,"* Mason stressed. *"We're doing our best to provide a stable home for Lucas."*

"I can see that." Ms. Chapman didn't seem to notice how much cleaning Aubrey had done in preparation for today. *"And really, all that matters is that Lucas is safe and happy."*

I am, Lucas signed with emphasis. *Does this mean I can stay?*

"Yes, I see no reason to move you to a new home." Ms. Chapman smiled and glanced at Aubrey. *"We will still do*

the occasional unannounced home visit, but I don't think you have anything to worry about."

"I have a question," Mason interjected. "*Would changing our address cause a problem for Lucas?*"

Aubrey frowned. "*What are you talking about?*"

"*My house is bigger,*" Mason pointed out. "*It's just a question.*"

"*Your address can change as long as Lucas has a bedroom of his own. The actual location itself shouldn't be a problem,*" Ms. Chapman assured him.

Aubrey winced because she knew Mason had been sleeping on the sofa for three weeks without complaint. No wonder he'd asked about a change in address. Although it irked her that he hadn't run the idea of moving past her.

The more she thought about it, the madder she became. It wasn't fair to spring that on her in the middle of an important meeting about Lucas's fate. About her future! She answered the next few questions from Ms. Chapman, then escorted the social worker to the door.

After the woman was gone, she swung to face Mason. "*When were you going to talk to me about moving? I'm not interested in relocating, I like being close to the Stanley School for the Deaf.*"

Mason smiled, came over, and dropped to one knee. She blinked as he held out a diamond engagement ring. "*Aubrey, I love you. Will you please do me the honor of becoming my wife?*"

She noticed Lucas was watching their interaction with rapt attention. The ring was beautiful, but that really wasn't the point. "*You can't propose while we're having an argument.*"

"*I love you,*" he repeated. "*Will you please marry me? There's no reason to argue, where we live isn't important as long as we're together. We can buy a new house in this area if that makes you happy. But I think we need a bigger house, and you have to admit, having a pool would be great for Lucas.*"

Her anger dissipated. He wasn't just trying to distract her. Maybe he had been his usual bossy self, but he was sincerely proposing. How could she resist? "*Oh, Mason. I love you too. I'd be honored to become your wife.*"

"*That's all that matters.*" Mason slipped the ring on the third finger of her left hand, then stood and drew her into his arms. He kissed her as if he might never stop.

And maybe wouldn't have if not for Lucas's snickering.

"Nothing like having a built-in chaperone," she whispered in Mason's right ear.

"Marry me soon, will you?" Mason whispered back. "Please?"

"Deal." She kissed him again, reveling in the strength of his arms, the warmth of his chest, and the love that they shared.

This was God's plan for them. And she couldn't be happier.

I HOPE you enjoyed Aubrey and Mason's story in *Sealed with Courage*. Are you ready for *Sealed with Honor*? If you'd like to read Kaleb and Charlotte's story, click here!

DEAR READER

Welcome to my new Called to Protect series! All my heroes are former Navy SEALs who find adventure and danger even living as civilians, and they find love. I hope you enjoyed *Sealed with Courage* and decide to give Kaleb's story a try. *Sealed with Honor* will be available soon. My goal is to have all six of these stories finished before the end of the year.

If you liked this book, please consider leaving a review. Reviews are critical for authors, and I would really appreciate your time. Thank you!

I also adore hearing from my readers. Without you, I wouldn't have any reason to write books. I can be found on Facebook at https://www.facebook.com/LauraScottBooks, on Twitter at https://twitter.com/laurascottbooks, on Instagram at https://www.instagram.com/laurascottbooks, and through my website at https://www.laurascottbooks.com. You may want to consider signing up for my monthly newsletter too. Not only will you find out when my new books are available, but I also offer an exclusive novella to all subscribers. This book is not available for sale on any venue.

Until next time,

Laura Scott

PS: If you're interested in taking a sneak peek of *Sealed with Honor*, I've included the first chapter here.

SEALED WITH HONOR

Chapter One

Retired Navy SEAL Kaleb Tyson knelt in the shadows with his black pit bull–lab mix, Sierra at his side. The dog provided a sense of calm as he studied the building the slim dark-haired woman had entered.

The structure was plain and appeared abandoned, yet he knew it wasn't. He'd followed Charlotte Cambridge, a big name for such a tiny woman, to this location twice now, and what little intel he'd gathered made him believe the place was a safe house for battered women and children.

A guy like him wouldn't be welcome, and the last thing he wanted was to frighten any of residents who had a right to their safety and privacy. But after weeks of digging into the last phone call Ava Rampart had made before she'd disappeared, he finally had something solid to go on.

Ava, the younger sister of their SEAL teammate Jaydon, had been missing for just over a month. Jaydon hadn't survived their last mission, but they'd brought his body home for a proper burial. The SEAL motto was no man left behind.

Dead or alive, they brought their teammates home.

Their team leader, Senior Chief Mason Gray, had taken the loss personally, but Kaleb knew they'd done their best. It wasn't anyone's fault that the op had gone sideways, especially since the rest of the team had barely escaped with their lives. And had sustained the injuries to prove it.

He idly rubbed his right knee, the one that had been reconstructed after that mission. A total knee replacement at forty years old didn't bode well for his future. A bum knee and debilitating headaches and nightmares were his personal souvenirs from that op. Sierra helped keep him grounded, which was how he found himself casing out the safe house located in a low-income area of Los Angeles, California.

When Kaleb glimpsed a man approaching the building, all his senses went on alert. Staying in the shadows, he pulled his Sig Sauer from its holster. Sierra stayed at his side as he lightly ran along the edge of the building to approach the stranger from behind. His knee twinged, but he ignored it and focused on the perp in front of him. Like him, the guy was dressed in black from head to toe.

Unlike him, though, the guy wore an ugly expression on his face and seemed intent on causing trouble. Kaleb didn't know for sure if the guy was armed, but he didn't discount the possibility.

Sierra wasn't a fully trained K9 yet, but thankfully, she didn't bark much. He'd worked with her often enough over these past few months that she understood basic hand signal commands. Kaleb dropped to a crouch twenty feet behind the guy and gave her a quick hand signal. Sierra sat beside him.

Adjusting to life as a civilian hadn't been easy. Unfortunately, he couldn't just shoot the guy, so he waited and watched.

The moment he saw the guy aim a gun at the door, Kaleb jumped to his feet. "Hey! Stop!"

A loud shot echoed as the bullet entered the doorjamb. Then the guy spun and ran. Kaleb grimaced and took off after him, praying his knee would hold up. The guy had a head start, disappearing behind another building.

By the time Kaleb reached it, there was no sign of him. He scanned the area, feeling certain the guy wasn't too far away. Then he thought about the safe house being breached and turned back.

The women and children would be vulnerable to another attack now that the doorjamb had been shattered. As he approached, he slowed when he saw the dark-haired woman standing in the doorway.

Even more surprising was the gun she held in her right hand.

The image of the tiny woman holding the gun almost made him want to smile. He didn't. Instead, he holstered his own weapon and raised his hands. "Ms. Cambridge? My name is Kaleb Tyson, and I'm a friend of Ava Rampart's brother. I saw the man who tried to break in and ran after him, but unfortunately, I lost him."

Charlotte Cambridge stared at him, keeping her weapon aimed at the center of his chest. "I've called the police."

"Good, that's smart." Kaleb nodded. Sierra lifted her nose to sniff the air. "I'm not here to harm anyone, I'm looking for Ava. She's missing, and her family is worried about her."

"Ava's not here." Charlotte didn't so much as waver in

her stance. "You best be on your way before the cops arrive."

"Okay, except I saw the guy who shot at your door." He kept his tone low-key and reasonable. "I'm happy to tell the police what I know."

"That's up to you." She looked as if she didn't care what happened to him. "I hope you have a permit for that gun."

"I do." Again, he wanted to grin. She looked like a tiny dynamo standing there, lecturing him on gun safety while holding him at gunpoint. "The guy who tried to get inside was roughly six feet tall, dark hair, and clean-shaven. He wore a black jacket and black jeans. The gun was a thirty-eight I believe, although I can't say for certain." Good thing his Sig Sauer wouldn't be a match to the bullet they dug out of the door.

"Why are you still here?" Charlotte asked, showing a tinge of annoyance.

"I told you, I'm looking for Ava Rampart. Her brother, Jaydon, was a member of our SEAL team."

"Was?"

Regret creased his features. "He didn't make it through the last op."

Charlotte surprised him by nodding. "Yeah, she mentioned that."

"So, Ava was here at one point." Finally, some common ground. The wail of sirens grew louder now, and he glanced over his shoulder expecting them to careen around the corner any minute. "I promise I'm not a threat to you or the other women staying there. I truly just want to find Ava."

Red and blue lights flashed from two squads heading toward them. Charlotte finally lowered her weapon. "How did you know we were here?"

He swallowed hard, trying to think of a response that

wouldn't alarm her. "I traced Ava's call to you, Ms. Cambridge. I must admit, it took me a while to find you."

She scowled. "It's not good that you found me at all," she snapped. Then she glanced at the damaged doorjamb. "Or that anyone else did either."

He wanted to reassure her that he hadn't given her away, but the officers approached from their respective squads, holding their weapons aimed at him. "Are you Charlotte Cambridge? Did you report gunfire?"

"Yes," she admitted.

"I'm a witness," Kaleb added calmly. "My name is Kaleb Tyson, and I'm a retired Navy SEAL. This is my K9 partner, Sierra." He used his chin to point at the dog since he still held his hands in the air. "I saw a white guy approach the door and then fire the weapon at the door handle. I shouted at him to stop, but he took off. Sierra and I followed, but unfortunately, we lost him." He glanced at Charlotte. "I didn't go too far because I was worried about the security breach here putting the residents in danger. I wanted to be sure there wasn't a second guy hiding in the wings."

A hint of appreciation flashed across Charlotte's features before she turned toward the officers. "I reported a man following me a few days ago," she informed them. "I spoke to a Detective Karl Grimes."

"And you're sure it's not this guy?" One of the officers gestured to him.

"I'm sure. The man following me has dark hair, not blond."

"Who is he?" Kaleb asked with a frown. "An ex-husband or boyfriend?"

Charlotte shrugged. "Probably, but no one I know. Likely an ex of one of the women seeking shelter here." Her expression turned grim. "I'm not happy this safe house has been compromised."

One of the cops patted him down, took his Sig and his MK3 knife, then asked to see his driver's license and gun permit. He handed them over, and the officer eyed them for a moment. "Kaleb with a K?"

"Yes." He got that response a lot.

"Hmm." The officer took them back to the squad, no doubt to run a background check.

He wasn't worried, considering he'd spent the past twenty-two years in the navy, there hadn't been any time to get into trouble with the law. However, he was concerned about Charlotte's safe house. "I'm happy to stick around to keep an eye on things."

She lifted a brow. "No men allowed inside."

He met her gaze squarely. "I didn't say anything about staying inside. Sierra and I can protect the place from out here."

She looked surprised at his offer but didn't say anything as another officer examined the door. "The slug is embedded in the doorframe. We'll have our crime scene techs dig it out and send it for evidence."

"Thank you," Charlotte murmured.

"You're clear," the cop said as he returned with Kaleb's license and permit. "Thanks for your service to our country."

"Ah, you're welcome." He appreciated the sentiment but was always caught off guard when someone said that to him. Especially after that last mission had gone so wrong. Jaydon was the one who'd given the ultimate sacrifice.

More reason for them to find his younger sister, Ava.

Which brought him back to Charlotte. She'd already admitted Ava had spent time there, but he needed more. He wanted to know everything Ava had said and done while she'd been there.

Charlotte Cambridge wouldn't like it, but he wasn't going anywhere. Not until he had answers.

And until he'd ensured her safety and that of the other women inside from whoever had shot at the safe house with the intent to get inside to harm them.

———

THE TALL HANDSOME man wasn't the guy who'd followed her before, but that didn't mean Charlotte didn't find him alarming.

She'd come a long way from those days she'd been a resident at a safe house much like the one she currently operated, but there were times she still felt vulnerable.

Kaleb with a K Tyson was a large, imposing man. Granted, he'd been nothing but respectful and forthright from the moment she'd spotted him, but she knew all too well that looks and actions could be deceiving.

Hadn't Jerry been sweet and considerate at first? Charming beyond belief, until the moment he'd punched her in the face. Only to turn around to claim it was her fault.

No. Charlotte gave herself a mental shake. This wasn't the time to traipse down memory lane. There was no point in reliving the past. She'd need all her energy to deal with this new threat.

The dark-haired man Kaleb had described sounded like the guy she'd glimpsed following her a few days ago. Obviously, there was no way to know for sure, but the fact that a dark-haired man had shot at the door to the safe house, likely intending to enter, was too much of a coincidence.

Swallowing a wave of helplessness, she focused on what needed to be done. There were ten women and four children inside who deserved to be safe. She could fix the broken door, but what if the dark-haired guy showed up again later?

Her gaze darted toward Kaleb. He'd offered to stand guard, remaining outside the building despite the cold weather. Not that winter in LA was anything like where she'd grown up in Minnesota. Still, she believed he'd meant what he'd said. That he'd stay outside to protect them.

"What's going on?"

Charlotte turned to see Milly, their live-in housekeeper, hovering behind her. Milly was only about ten years Charlotte's senior, but she took on a motherly role to her and their residents.

"The police are here; we're fine. Nothing to be concerned about." She did her best to reassure Milly.

"Did they catch the man who shot at us?" Milly planted her hands on her plump hips.

"Not yet." Considering they didn't have much of a description to go on, Charlotte doubted they would find him anytime soon. Unless, of course, he showed up again. "Please keep everyone calm, okay? We're safe."

"Are we?" Milly stared at her for a moment before turning away. "I know the drill," she muttered as she returned to the main living quarters.

Charlotte let out a sigh. She couldn't blame Milly or the others for being afraid. She'd done everything possible to avoid being followed here, but it must not have been enough.

Why couldn't these men just leave them alone? As if it wasn't enough to terrorize women and children once, but to keep looking for them after they were gone? She didn't understand the mentality of these guys who risked everything to seek revenge.

"Ms. Cambridge?" She swung to face Kaleb, who'd managed to approach so silently she hadn't heard him. She put a hand on her chest to calm her racing heart. "Will you allow me to fix your door?"

Far be it for her to turn down a helping hand. She glanced at his black dog, then back at him. "I have a toolbox and supplies inside. If you wouldn't mind waiting out here?"

"Yes, ma'am."

"Call me Charlotte." She was thirty-seven years old, feeling more like seventy-seven without the added ma'ams and Ms. Cambridges. Besides, she believed he was honestly here out of concern for Ava. A fear she privately shared, especially after Ava disappeared from the safe house without telling her or Milly where she was going.

Something she'd have to let Kaleb know, sooner rather than later. But not until the door was repaired.

Charlotte whirled away to get what he'd need. She returned with the toolbox and extra two-by-fours.

"Thank you." Kaleb had a flashlight out and was examining the door frame. "I can see why he used a gun, no way to get inside otherwise."

"That's the point." She crossed her arms over her chest, chilled from the cool night air.

"Do you have cameras?" Kaleb stepped back to look above the doorframe.

"No," she admitted. "This is generally a temporary housing location. Residents stay only for a couple of weeks before being handed off to another location."

"You need cameras. I'll get some tomorrow." He moved

to the side to make room for the crime scene tech. "You need motion sensor lights too."

She stared at him for a moment. "We bring victims here during the night and would prefer not to announce our location, so no lights. Besides, the outside of the building is supposed to look abandoned, not wired for sound."

"They have really small cameras, I can mount them out of view." He scanned the building. "I get your point about the lights, but I still think it's better to have them than not. Especially now."

She tried not to feel depressed. "We'll have to find a new location soon anyway, so there's no point in doing all of that." The idea of moving was daunting, although it wasn't the first time.

And probably wouldn't be the last.

"Got it." The crime scene tech held up the slug with a triumphant look. "Mangled pretty bad, but I'd say it's a thirty-eight."

She nodded. Her gun was a small thirty-eight as well. She practiced shooting targets every two weeks and had gotten very good. Her instructor had warned her, though, that shooting at paper silhouettes was very different from aiming and firing at a person. Still, she knew she would do whatever was necessary to keep these women safe.

The officers left shortly after the crime scene tech had gotten their evidence, leaving her and Kaleb alone.

"This won't take long." He hefted the two-by-four into place.

She stepped back to give him room to work. He seemed to know what he was doing, and soon the door was repaired so that it would close properly.

"We'll need to replace the handle and lock, but that will need to wait until morning." Kaleb pushed the toolbox inside. "Don't worry, though. I'll stay out here with Sierra. We won't let anyone get close."

"You can't stay out there all night," she protested.

He arched a brow. "I'll be fine for another eight to nine hours."

It was already midnight, and Charlotte knew she should just let him stay outside as promised. But she couldn't do it. "It's too cold. You can stay inside, but only in the hallway."

"I don't want to cause anxiety for your residents." He glanced at his dog. "Sierra and I can huddle together to stay warm."

"Please, Kaleb. I'll just worry about you out here." She glanced over her shoulder. "I'll reassure our residents, and as long as you stay in the hallway, they should be fine."

A grin tugged at the corner of his mouth. "It's sweet that you're worried, but I've stayed in far worse conditions. And out here, I can see the threat coming before it arrives." He hesitated, then added, "I wouldn't say no to a cup of coffee, though, if it's not too much trouble."

She realized he wasn't kidding about staying outside in the cold. Slowly, she nodded. "No trouble at all. Give me a few minutes to brew a pot, okay?"

"Thanks." His grin widened, and she had to look away from his ridiculously handsome features.

The man no doubt had dozens of women who'd chased after him all his life. He wasn't wearing a wedding ring, but that didn't mean anything. Charlotte reminded herself she was immune to good-looking men. Jerry had been the best cure around.

But her stomach still knotted with awareness when she returned with a large insulated mug of coffee for him. Just handing it over seemed to bring her far too close for comfort. "I—uh, should have asked if you wanted cream and sugar."

"None of that available in the Middle East," he said dryly. "Black is just fine. Thanks."

"I—um, thanks again. For doing this." She'd never felt so awkward in a man's presence as she did at that moment. Honestly, maybe she was out of practice, but still. There was no reason to overreact. It wasn't as if Kaleb was sticking around. Once he'd learned what he could about Ava's time there, he'd be on his merry way.

"Do you have a minute to talk about Ava?" He regarded her thoughtfully. "How long ago did she leave here?"

She hesitated, then decided she wouldn't be putting Ava in more danger by talking to him. The woman had left under her own free will. The safe house wasn't a jail, the women could leave if they wanted. Although once they did, they weren't allowed back to the same place. They'd have to go somewhere else.

"We're worried about her," Kaleb said when she didn't answer.

"We?"

He nodded. "The rest of Jaydon's team. Nico in particular was Jaydon's swim buddy. He's very worried about Ava and is trying to find her boyfriend, the one she supposedly left with six weeks ago."

"How many team members?" She flushed, hoping he didn't think she was being too nosy. "Never mind, I suppose that doesn't matter."

"Six of us," he replied. "Although right now, it's just me and Nico searching for Ava."

She nodded. "She left this safe house two weeks ago. I'm not sure why, she didn't confide in me. Or Milly."

"And Milly is?"

"Our live-in housekeeper, although all the women living

here have chores to do. It helps to keep them busy. Idle hands and all of that."

"Two weeks." He sighed and rubbed the back of his neck. "If I'd have gotten here sooner . . ."

"Don't play the what-if game," she said quickly. "That's something I'm constantly preaching to the women who seek shelter here. None of us can go back and change the past, no matter how much we wish we could. All we can do is to move forward."

"God's plan is not ours to question," he murmured.

She was surprised to hear him say that. Their safe house was supported financially by several Christian organizations, for which she was extremely grateful. Yet she hadn't been able to fully embrace the concept of God when seeing so many women and children suffering. "Yes, well, I—uh should get inside. Good night."

"Good night, Charlotte." His husky voice washed over her. She turned and nearly walked face-first into the doorjamb he'd just repaired.

Feeling all kinds of foolish, she closed the door and leaned against it.

"What's wrong, Charlotte?" Emma, a sweet young woman barely twenty, padded toward her. "Milly said we're safe, but you look worried."

She pushed her emotions aside to smile reassuringly at Emma. "We are safe, I promise. We have a bodyguard stationed outside to watch over us."

"A bodyguard?" Emma repeated, her daze darting from Charlotte to the door behind her. "Can we trust him?"

It broke Charlotte's heart that these women had lost their ability to trust anyone, especially men. Between drug and alcohol abuse and general unhappiness with their lives, too many men had taken their anger and frustration out on those they were supposed to protect the most. Their women and children.

The violence never ceased to confound her, even though she'd experienced it firsthand. "Yes, Emma, we can trust him. Our bodyguard served our country as a Navy SEAL. He'll protect us tonight. And tomorrow, I'll make arrangements to move us to a new location."

Emma nodded and turned away. Charlotte watched the young woman return to the living area, then let out a soundless sigh.

She'd truly believed they were safe here for what was left of the night.

It was only after Kaleb left that they'd have to worry about the dark-haired man finding them again.